**"Will you dry the back of my hair for me?"
Sacha asked.**

He didn't answer for a moment. "Hand me the dryer." He swung his feet to the floor on each side of her as he reached for it.

She closed her eyes in purely sensual pleasure as the soft warm air caressed her nape and Brody's fingers combed through the damp tresses. His bare legs were cradling her between them. Brody really had beautiful legs, she thought dreamily. She'd known he looked great in tights, but uncovered they looked far more virile and brawny.

"Are you falling asleep?" Brody asked.

"No, I was just thinking about what a nice body you have." She leaned her head against his chest. His skin felt deliciously rough against her flesh and she rubbed her cheek back and forth with catlike pleasure, enjoying the textures of him.

"Stop that!" Brody's voice was charged with tension.

She chuckled. "Am I tickling you?"

He groaned. He'd never be able to sleep tonight. . . .

WHAT ARE *LOVESWEPT* ROMANCES?

They are stories of true romance and touching emotion. We believe those two very important ingredients are constants in our highly sensual and very believable stories in the *LOVESWEPT* line. Our goal is to give you, the reader, stories of consistently high quality that may sometimes make you laugh, sometimes make you cry, but are always fresh and creative and contain many delightful surprises within their pages.

Most romance fans read an enormous number of books. Those they truly love, they keep. Others may be traded with friends and soon forgotten. We hope that each *LOVESWEPT* romance will be a treasure—a "keeper." We will always try to publish

LOVE STORIES YOU'LL NEVER FORGET
BY AUTHORS YOU'LL ALWAYS REMEMBER

The Editors

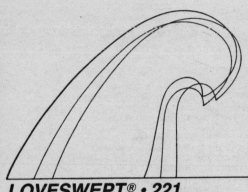

LOVESWEPT® • 221

Iris Johansen
The Spellbinder

BANTAM BOOKS
TORONTO • NEW YORK • LONDON • SYDNEY • AUCKLAND

THE SPELLBINDER
A Bantam Book / November 1987

If you would be interested in receiving protective vinyl covers for your Loveswept books, please write to this address for information:

Loveswept
Bantam Books
P.O. Box 985
Hicksville, NY 11802

ISBN 0-553-21855-7

Published simultaneously in the United States and Canada

Bantam Books are published by Bantam Books, Inc. Its trademark, consisting of the words "Bantam Books" and the portrayal of a rooster, is Registered in U.S. Patent and Trademark Office and in other countries. Marca Registrada. Bantam Books, Inc., 666 Fifth Avenue, New York, New York 10103.

One

Brody Devlin appeared on stage to take his eighth curtain call.

The applause swelled, redoubling in volume as it echoed off the walls of the huge old theater. Every person in the audience was on his feet. His most ardent fans were wild with enthusiasm. They wanted to cling to him, keep him within their field of vision, listen to his deep, mesmerizing voice speak any words that would continue to envelop them in the spell he had been weaving about them all evening.

Spellbinder.

The word jumped suddenly into Sacha's mind. For two months she had been trying to analyze Brody Devlin's power over audiences; now she realized there was no logical explanation. He was a phenomenon, an actor who exuded such power and presence, he quite simply hypnotized and charmed, changing impossibility into reality, the commonplace into high drama. Even in this lightweight revival of the musical *Camelot* his power was riveting.

Of course, his magnificent good looks were an asset that couldn't be discounted. His role was demanding. He should have been exhausted now. But that didn't seem to be the case. He stood center stage, and from where Sacha was watching in the tenth row, she felt as though she were absorbing some of the crackling energy he radiated. In the dark green velvet of his medieval costume he looked so stunning, one reviewer had said it was an accolade to his acting that he could make King Arthur believable as a cuckolded husband. Devlin's shoulder-length hair was a deep chestnut color and his tall, broad-shouldered, slim-hipped physique conveyed an impression of tough yet magnetically appealing sexuality. The camera loved his face, but not because he had the features of an Adonis. His brilliant blue eyes were wide set and tilted up slightly at the corners, and his broad cheekbones and short nose were definitely irregular as was his long sensual mouth. Yet put them together, and they combined to create a face to fascinate and beguile. The face of a spellbinder.

But tonight those brilliant blue eyes seemed restless and the smile on his tanned face betrayed impatience. Sacha inhaled sharply as she recognized the sign for which she had been watching for the past week: There was an air of leashed tension about him. Tonight. It would be tonight.

Sacha turned to Louis. "Call your contact at the reception desk of his hotel," she said in an urgent whisper, "and tell him it will be tonight. Probably within the next hour or so."

Louis Benoit raised an inquiring brow. "You're sure? Jason is a very greedy man. He will charge us even if you're wrong."

Sacha glanced back at the man on the stage. Devlin's tension was growing. She could sense it even as the actor, masking it with a careless, charming smile, bowed and waved to the audience. "I'm sure. Hurry."

Louis nodded and then moved rapidly past the other people in their row. He hurried up the aisle, trying to get ahead of the crowd, which would be converging on the exits as soon as Brody released them from his spell.

Devlin would not be persuaded to come back after this curtain call, Sacha thought. No matter how loudly people in the audience clamored for him to return, he wouldn't. Sacha had studied him so closely for the last two months that she felt as if she knew his every thought. And tonight, she felt certain, he would tell Cass to make the arrangements.

Cold perspiration dampened her palms, and she wiped them on her jeans. It was unusual for her to be nervous, but now she was more frightened than the first time Gino had sent her out on the streets. She drew a deep breath and braced herself, deliberately trying to subdue the apprehension that could make a coward of her. She had learned a long time ago that worrying never accomplished anything. It was better just to make up your mind, do what you set out to do with as much verve and style as you were capable of, and keep smiling. By assuming a cheerful outlook you could sometimes fool even yourself into believing everything was all right.

She was only nervous now because tonight was terribly important to her and she had waited for such a long time for it. She would be fine as soon as she swung into action, she assured herself.

Devlin was leaving the stage. It was the signal for her to depart too. She snatched up her worn blue-jean jacket from the back of the seat and slipped it on, her gaze still clinging to Brody Devlin as he strode gracefully toward the wings.

As soon as he disappeared from view she started to move toward the aisle, excusing herself to the beautifully dressed patrons who were still applauding loudly, hoping for Devlin to appear again. She was scarcely aware of the condescending and surprised looks her faded jeans and scuffed loafers received. She was too intent on getting out and catching a taxi to take her to the hotel to worry about how she looked. Not that she would have worried anyway. You wore what you had the money to buy, and then, if anyone looked down his nose at you, you found a way to tweak that nose—again with the utmost style.

Sacha hurried out of the theater and took a

deep breath. The fresh air was invigorating after the perfumed closeness of the auditorium and, she noted, surprisingly cool for March in San Diego.

Damn, she didn't have much money left after buying those tickets tonight, and it was only a few blocks to the hotel. Maybe, if she hurried, she could walk it and still . . . No, she couldn't take the chance. Tonight was too important. She jumped into the first waiting taxi in the zone in front of the theater and leaned forward to speak to the driver. "Ventura Hotel. Hurry, please."

Brody was unbuttoning his emerald velvet doublet even as he reached the wings. He accepted the hot drink Joel Morton, the stagehand, held out to him and swallowed it in three swift gulps. Damn, he hated hot lemon juice. He would be glad to have this tour over so that he didn't have to go through the motions of pampering his nonexistent singing voice. Then he could relax and—

And what? Lie on the beach at Malibu and vegetate? Better hot juice and road tours like this than the boredom that besieged him when he wasn't working at all. He handed the glass back to the stagehand. "I want to see Cass," he said curtly as he turned and strode down the hall to his dressing room.

Joel Morton pursed his lips in a low whistle. Devlin's notorious temper was obviously about to go on the rampage. It was completely out of character for him to be short with any member of the crew or with minor cast members. He usually saved his scathing sarcasm and glacier stares for the professionals in his own league. Well, Joel thought, it wasn't his job to cope with Devlin's displeasure. He'd deliver the summons to Cass Radison, Devlin's manager, and let him try to calm down the actor.

Brody slammed the door of his dressing room, tersely dismissed his dresser, Chuck, shrugged out of the velvet doublet, and threw it on the top of the screen across the room. He sat down before the mirror and began taking off his stage makeup with swift, jerky movements.

There was a perfunctory knock on the door before Cass opened it and strolled into the dressing room. "A great performance, Brody."

"How do you know? You never watch the show and you have a tin ear." Brody threw a soiled tissue into the wastecan. "I was flat as hell in at least half my numbers tonight."

"Strange, the audience didn't seem to notice it," Cass observed mildly. "You must have done something right." He dropped down into the easy chair by the door. "Or maybe they just liked your costumes. You've got great legs in those tights."

A reluctant smile tugged at Brody's lips as he met Cass's limpidly innocent brown-eyed gaze in the mirror. "Thanks, I can always count on you to pinpoint my more stellar qualities." He stood up and began unbuttoning his white balloon-sleeved shirt. "Not that I displayed many tonight. I don't know why I took this role. I stink."

"That's not what *Time* and *People* magazines said."

"I can't sing. The role has no dimension. I should have done *Tempest* at the Old Vic."

"You did Shakespeare last year. You thought this would be a challenge."

Brody pulled the tails of his shirt out of the loden-green tights. "Did I? I don't remember." He stripped the shirt off and tossed it beside the doublet over the screen. "I was wrong." He went to the closet, found the street clothes his dresser had readied for him and tossed them on the chair before the dressing table. "Thank God this is the last week."

"Have you read those film scripts I gave you?"

Brody nodded. "One has possibilities. I'll let you know."

Cass rose to his feet, his lanky body surprisingly graceful. "Hungry? I'll call a car and we'll find a decent restaurant. I feel like Chinese."

Brody shook his head. "Not tonight." He resumed undressing. "Call Marceline's service and have them send someone to the hotel."

There was no surprise in Cass's face. He had been half expecting the order. He knew Brody was extremely highly sexed, and this request usually came at least once or twice in every town they played. "Same type as usual?"

Brody nodded.

"Right away." Cass turned and opened the door.

"Are you sure you don't want to give our resident nymphomaniac, Guenevere, a try instead? She has all the requirements. She's blond, stacked, and I understand she has a bedroom repertoire that would put any call girl to shame. I notice she's done everything but crawl into your bed since she took over the lead in Saint Louis."

"You're behind the times." Brody smiled cynically. "She did that in Denver."

Cass looked mildly surprised. "Really? What did you do?"

"Tossed her out on her fanny. The last thing I need is an affair with a bitch like Naomi Marlow; that would really complete the idiocy of this tour."

Cass nodded. No complications. It was the creed Brody lived by these days. Yet Brody was a very complicated man himself and that did breed more complexities. Catch-22. His father had been a much easier client to deal with when Cass had been his manager. Perhaps it was to be expected. Raymond Devlin had never been more than a fine character actor; Brody had reached superstardom when he was only twenty-five and had maintained that status for the last ten years. Brody had been offered every plum life had to offer and had tasted most of them. Cass supposed it was natural that the actor's palate had become jaded. He was the darling of film and stage, acclaimed the greatest actor since Olivier, and had been chased by women in every country.

Through it all he had remained surprisingly levelheaded, and each success had only fanned the desire to better his next performance, increase his range, bring something new and fresh to each succeeding role. Still, Brody's search for perfection didn't make Cass's job any easier. The actor could be demanding, single-minded, and scathing if he detected any lack of professionalism in the people surrounding him. Cass had no problem with that aspect of his character; it was balanced by a sense of fairness and the generosity to give whatever help was needed to reach the common goal of any production.

However, many people in the business didn't share Cass's view, and Brody's ruthlessness had been as highly publicized as his many affairs. Well, that was their hang-up, Cass reasoned. He liked Brody as a man and respected him as an artist. He just wished to hell that the man would stop asking quite so much of himself and the people around him so they could all be more comfortable. Cass was getting too old for challenges. "I'll call the service and tell them to have a woman in your suite when you get there."

"Good." Brody strode naked toward the bathroom door. "Thanks, Cass."

"Just one of my wide array of services," Cass said lightly. "One I've perfected over the years."

Brody stopped with his hand on the doorknob to gaze curiously at his manager. "I've never asked you. Did you perform this particular service for my father too?"

Cass shook his head. "He preferred amateurs

and wasn't nearly as fastidious as you about complications."

Brody's lips twisted. "So I've heard." He had scarcely known his father. He was the child of Raymond's second marriage and had visited him rarely during his lifetime. Raymond Devlin had been divorced four times and been involved in innumerable well-publicized affairs before his death eight years before. "To each his own."

Two minutes after the door closed behind Cass, Brody was under the shower. The warm water whipping against his body should have been soothing, but it failed to ease the tension knotting his muscles. Once he had reached this point, not even sex could totally relieve it. It was too raw and abrasive to yield to sleep or exercise, and he wasn't stupid enough to use drugs or liquor. If he could just hold on until he got back to the hotel, the woman in the suite should help. He would sink into her body and take the edge off both his abstinence and this damn tension, which was almost always with him. He should have sent for a woman before this but he had felt an unaccountable reluctance. He thought it might have something to do with the boredom that had been gnawing at him for the past few years. Bored with sex? He must be getting old. No, his physical arousal was as strong as ever. It was the emptiness he felt afterward that bothered him.

Still, sex helped more than anything else to defeat his nemesis. The tension would return after the act, but it wouldn't be this bad for a while.

He would be fine as soon as he got to his suite and saw the woman.

He closed his eyes, thinking about the woman Marceline would send, and let the water pour over him. His instructions were always the same. The call girl must be blond, voluptuous, and versatile. She was given a key by the desk clerk and was always waiting naked in bed when he arrived at the suite.

The woman wasn't blond, she wasn't voluptuous, and she definitely wasn't waiting naked in bed.

She was sitting fully dressed in the cane chair in the sitting room and jumped to her feet as soon as he opened the door. "Hello." Her voice was breathless. "I'm Sacha Lorion. I'm very happy to meet you."

The words held the faintest hint of an accent of some kind. French? Well, it didn't matter. She was all wrong. What the hell could the service have been thinking of to send someone like this teenage Lolita to him? She looked about seventeen in those beat-up jeans and jacket, and she was staring at him with the fearless wide-eyed curiosity of a much younger child.

"I'm Brody Devlin and I'm afraid there's been a mistake. You're not what I wanted."

"No?" She moistened her lips with her tongue. "You don't like me?"

The accent *was* French, and her husky voice was vaguely erotic, Brody noted, stroking him like a whisper in the dark. Maybe . . . No, conversation was seldom required from his partners, and he would feel guilty as hell taking this big-eyed child to bed. "You're too young," he said gently.

"I'm twenty-one."

He should have known Marceline's service wouldn't deal with children. Marceline's women were all skilled professionals of the highest order. No doubt some of her customers preferred the kinky imagery of bedding a budding nymphet, but she would never risk supplying the actual goods. He closed the door behind him. "I'm sorry, you still won't do."

"You think I'm ugly? I know I'm not to everyone's taste." The question was asked with no coyness, only that same bold curiosity he had noted in her expression.

"No, you're actually quite . . . attractive." It wasn't the right word, but her appeal was difficult to categorize. Her skin was truly magnificent, Brody thought, rose petals on velvet. Her ebony hair shone clean and healthy in the lamplight, falling to her shoulders and curving under in a simple page boy to frame high cheekbones, slightly pouty lips, and light blue eyes faintly uptilted at the corners. There was something vaguely familiar about those eyes, he thought absently. "I'm afraid you're just not my type."

She smiled and he inhaled sharply. Not attractive. Beautiful. Her face was suddenly illuminated from within by a warmth and vitality that was near incandescent. "Then of course, I won't do at all," she said cheerfully. "I'm sorry. There must have been a mix-up. Don't worry, I'll take care of everything." She strode briskly toward the telephone on the desk in the far corner of the sitting room. "I'll call Marceline's right away and arrange for a replacement." She paused with her hand on the receiver and glanced back over her shoulder. "At this time of night it may take an hour or so, but I will take good care of you until she gets here. Have you eaten yet?"

"No, but—"

"Then I will cook you a fine meal." She made a shooing motion with one hand as she picked up the receiver with the other. "Go to your bedroom and rest. I know you must be tired after your performance tonight. I'll call you when the food is ready."

Brody felt his lips twitching with amusement. "Do you always supply chef service to your customers?"

"But you are not my customer." Sacha smiled sunnily. "You are a hungry man who has been badly treated by my employer. The least I can do is to see that you are fed and pampered *un peu*."

"You're French?"

She shook her head. "Hungarian mother, American father, but I grew up in Paris." She made another shooing motion. "You go rest. All will be well, I promise you."

Brody found himself meekly obeying her command. As the bedroom door closed behind him he took off his tan Windbreaker and tossed it on the bed. It was odd, but the tension and boredom gripping him had eased since he had entered the suite. The little Sacha had surprised and amused him, but he had definitely not been bored.

He sat down on the king-size bed and looked around in discontent. Why the devil had he let the woman banish him to the bedroom? He wasn't tired. The energy was coursing through him as it usually did after a performance.

"Brody?" The door opened and Sacha's gleaming, dark head poked around it. "I'm sorry, but I will need you in the kitchen. Those idiots in the hotel have stocked the refrigerator with only milk, eggs, cheese, and bacon." Her face lit with a gamine grin. "But all is not lost. I found"—she paused dramaticaly— "mushrooms. We will have a magnificent quiche, if you only dice the mushrooms while I brown the bacon."

He rose swiftly to his feet, feeling as if he had been reprieved. "I think I can manage that." He followed her to the small, gleaming kitchen, noticing she was taller than he had first thought. It must have been her slenderness that had created the illusion of lack of height. She had discarded her denim jacket, and he smothered a smile as he saw the pink T-shirt she wore had DISNEY WORLD printed on the back and a huge Donald Duck on the front. Lolita, indeed.

Then his amusement vanished as his gaze lingered on her small breasts, outlined with such loving detail by the T-shirt that it was evident she was wearing no bra. He had a sudden impulse to lift the shirt and cup her breasts in his hands.

That creamy rose tinting her cheeks was very alluring, and the texture fantastic. Would her nipples be as velvety as—

"There will be a replacement here as soon as possible," Sacha said. "Marceline's manager apologizes profusely and hopes you will accept any small service I can do for you until she can make reparation." She shot him a mischievous glance. "So you see, since she's paying me, you must let me make you comfortable. I regard it as my duty, and I always do my duty."

"Do you?" Annoyance as unreasonable as it was strong suddenly jabbed through him. His tone became caustic. "I bet you're damn good at those duties too."

Her smile faded, and he felt as if he'd slapped a child. "Sometimes. I try very hard." She motioned to the red plastic and chrome chair beside the Formica table. "If you will sit down, I will get you the mushrooms."

"Sacha . . ."

She glanced over her shoulder. "Yes?"

"I'm sorry." The words came haltingly. "That was uncalled for. Sometimes I can be a complete bastard."

She smiled. "Then we must work to correct that condition. Right?" She took a large bottle of mushrooms from the refrigerator, snatched up a cutting board from a hook on the wall and a paring knife from the drawer beneath the sink. She carried them to him and set the objects on the table. "If you do this job very well, I will consider it suitable penance." She met his gaze steadily. "And you are not a bastard, Brody. I think you could be very difficult, but that is a different thing entirely." She turned away, strode to the cabinet, and got down a mixing bowl. "Now, I must obviously feed you quickly. Probably hunger makes you bad-tempered."

He wasn't so sure. When he had thought of Sacha in bed with one of her nymphet-loving clients, he had experienced a surge of rage that had caught him off-guard. He found the image lingering distastefully even now. "Probably." He opened the jar of mushrooms. "I see by your T-shirt that you were at Walt Disney World. When did you go?"

"A few weeks ago." She was breaking eggs into the mixing bowl with economical efficiency. "I had a wonderful time. It's truly a magic place. Have you ever been there?"

He shook his head. "We played Orlando last month, but I didn't bother to go."

"You should have. I know you don't like crowds but—"

"How do you know that?" he asked idly.

She paused in the motion of breaking an egg. "I must have read it somewhere." She cracked the shell. "I know people recognize you wherever you go, and that must bother you, but you can't hide away when there are so many wonderful things to see."

It had been a long time since he had experienced the eagerness he saw in her face. He suddenly felt terribly old and cynical. "I'll see it next time." His gaze went to the front of her shirt. "You like Donald Duck?"

She nodded decisively. "Oh, yes. He's my favorite cartoon character, but I had trouble finding a shirt with his picture. Everything was Mickey Mouse. The salesgirl at the shop told me he was more popular." She scowled. "Bah! Who would like a meek, bland character like Mickey over Donald Duck?"

Bah? He didn't think he'd ever heard the expression outside of vintage movies, yet he found the word entirely natural and even charming coming from Sacha's lips. "Since Donald is irascible, crafty, vengeful, and underhanded, I could imagine a few misguided souls who might prefer Mickey."

"But he can also be affectionate and rather sweet, and it's no wonder he behaves badly when he's persecuted by those dreadful chipmunks. I feel quite sorry for him. He can't help it if he's difficult."

He chuckled. "You seem to make it a habit of forgiving difficult types. Not that I put myself in the same elite class as Donald."

She wrinkled her nose as she glanced at him over her shoulder. "It isn't kind of you to laugh at me. I'm entirely sincere. I can't help it if I've always found difficult people more worthwhile in the long run."

"Are you flattering me, Sacha?"

"Bah! I do not flatter. If I can't be honest, I do not speak at all." She paused. "Well, that's not exactly true. But if I lie, there's always a good reason."

The smile of amusement lingered on his lips. "I see."

"Are those mushrooms ready? You're being very slow."

"Sorry. I'll try to do better." He looked up. "In my job I don't get much practice at cooking."

"That's no excuse. In my job I don't either."

Another flash of burning irritation surprised him as a vividly obscene picture flashed through his mind. What the devil was wrong with him? She was a high-priced hooker who was obviously content with her profession. Why should he care who she slept with after she left him tonight? "Maybe you have an affinity for it," he said curtly, pushing the cutting board away. "I don't think I'm hungry after all. You eat the quiche when you've finished and then run along."

She turned to face him, her expression clouding. "What did I do wrong? I was enjoying myself, and I thought you were too. I thought we were being very . . . companionable."

He felt a flicker of remorse. It wasn't her fault he was being pricked by these weird emotions. "You didn't do anything wrong. And we were being very companionable."

"Then what . . . ?" She trailed off, looking at him pensively. "I know what it is. You didn't like it that I criticized you." Her expression softened. "I didn't mean to hurt you. I had no idea you were so sensitive. I will be careful not to do it again. You will stay?"

He was having trouble tearing his gaze away from her pleading face. It was getting out of hand. He couldn't remember ever responding to a woman on the multitude of levels he was to Sacha. Surprise, amusement, tenderness, and the burning possessiveness that had been bothering him whenever he thought of Sacha in bed with another man. Jealousy. Talk about dog in the manger. He couldn't desire this big-eyed street urchin.

Or could he? His body's arousal testified that he most definitely did want her, and the idea began to intrigue him. She was certainly different, and his reaction to her had been . . . unusual. Bedding her would undoubtedly be a change of pace and might lessen his boredom as well as that damn tension. He would have to think about it.

He sat back down and picked up the paring knife. "I'll stay." He smiled mockingly. "As long as you remember what a delicate, sensitive person I am behind this hard facade. Just like Donald Duck."

She looked a little uncertain before she nodded briskly. "I'll remember." She turned away. "And now I'll tell you all about Epcot, which will cause you to gnash your teeth with envy."

"When I was a little girl, I always wanted to go to an amusement park but I never—" Sacha glanced up from her plate, her fork poised in midair. "Why are you looking at me like that?"

"Like what?" Brody asked, leaning back in his chair and gazing at her innocently. "I was just thinking that you bake an excellent quiche."

She made a face. "And you were thinking, 'what a chatterbox she is'. I've talked your ear off for the last hour, and I've scarcely let you eat a bite. No wonder you look so hungry." She pointed to the half-eaten quiche on his plate. "*Mangez*. I will be still as a mouse."

"Mickey Mouse?"

She shook her head. "He talks too much. Maybe the mouse that ran up the clock."

"You're well versed in your nursery rhymes."

"I used to tell them to the other children at the—" She broke off. "If I'm the mouse, then the way you are looking at me is definitely feline. What are you thinking?"

He considered telling her that he had been imagining her lying naked on her back on the king-size bed down the hall, her thighs thrown open as he moved between them. He'd been having similar erotic visions all through the meal and found himself enjoying the anticipation of the act to come almost as much as he usually did the climax with any other woman. He decided he would stretch his anticipation just a little longer before he took Sacha to bed.

Besides, there was no hurry. He was enjoying their dinner on another level. Her conversation had been both relaxing and amusing, and he had found her bright, witty, and glowing with an enthusiasm that was very refreshing. "I was thinking I'd like another cup of coffee."

She raised a skeptical brow but stood up and crossed the room to the coffeemaker on a cabinet.

She had an intriguingly pert bottom, Brody thought appreciatively, and the jeans molded it quite satisfactorily. He would like to mold it himself, run his palm over that delicious curve, feel the muscles flex at his touch. Perhaps he would have her bend down and—

She was coming back to him, setting the cup before him with a bright smile. "Coffee. Now you must finish the quiche."

His hand closed on her wrist. It was time to end it. The muscles of his stomach were knotting, his groin swelling and aching. If he didn't get her into the bedroom soon, he'd be taking her on this kitchen chair. "Call Marceline's."

Her eyes widened in surprise. "But I told you that I already called her."

He swiveled around on the chair so that she was between his legs. She smelled of clean soap and something sweetly floral, and her skin was even more velvety up close. His hand on her wrist was trembling, he noticed in amazement. He tightened his grip until he could feel the birdlike fragility of bone beneath the soft skin. His thumb slowly stroked the inside of her wrist, feeling the pulse leap beneath his touch. "Call her back. Tell her I've changed my mind."

She seemed to be holding her breath. "You don't want a woman?"

He lifted her wrist to his lips and his tongue licked delicately at the tracery of blue veins beneath the thin skin. "I didn't say that. I just decided I'd like to try something different."

She was staring at him dumbfounded. "Different?"

His knees closed, holding her captive. He could feel the warmth of her beneath the layers of material separating them. To hell with going to the bedroom. "You," he said thickly. "Take off that damn Donald Duck shirt. I don't want him looking at me accusingly when I—"

"You want *me*?" Her voice was not only stunned, it was panic-stricken. "But you can't, that's not possible. You only like blondes."

His hand released her wrist and traveled around to cup the curve of her bottom. It felt as good as he had thought it would. "I don't want to get into a rut." His eyes twinkled. "Not that I'm unalterably opposed to that state. There are ruts and then there are ruts."

"I'm too thin. And I have very small breasts."

"Yes, and you have a fantastic derriere." He leaned forward, his open lips nuzzling her nipple through the T-shirt.

"No!" Her hands were on his shoulders, attempting to push away from him. "You aren't supposed to . . ." She backed away from him, her face aflame. "You can't do this."

"Try me." He stood up. "If there's a problem

about the other woman they're sending, tell Marceline I'll pay for both of you." He inched even closer. "She won't mind."

"You don't understand." Her hands went to her hot cheeks. "It wasn't supposed to be this way. I'm not the sort of woman you want. This is most disconcerting."

He frowned. "Why? This is why you came here, so don't start playing silly games."

"No games." One hand ran distractedly through the sleekness of her hair. "I don't know what to do."

"Well, I do. First, we take off Donald Duck. Then we sit down, and I—"

"No, it's impossible. You don't understand."

His smile faded. "You keep saying that," he said with soft menace. "What I do understand is that I've decided I want you, and you're acting like a damn whimpering virgin. I also understand that I'm getting mad as hell. Is there anything else I should understand?"

"Yes." She sighed resignedly. "One more thing."

"Would you care to enlighten me as to what that is?"

"I'm your sister."

Two

He went still. "Would you mind repeating that?"

"I'm your sister." She hurried on. "Your half sister, actually, but it's the same thing. We had the same father." He was gazing at her blankly. Oh damn, she hadn't wanted to tell him so soon. She had known he would react like this. "So you can see why I can't go to bed with you. It would be incest. Not that I would have gone to bed with you anyway. That wasn't what I had in mind at all. How was I to know you'd behave so out of character? I'm not the type of person you usually—"

"Hold it." He held up his hand to stem the flow of words. "Stop right there. What the hell are you doing here if you had no intention of going to bed with me?"

"That's not the question you should be asking,"

she said reprovingly. "I've just told you I'm your sister. That's far more important."

"You'll forgive me if I disagree," he said caustically. "You're not my sister, and at the moment, the fact you're not going to bed with me is as important as hell. I'm *hurting*, dammit."

Quick concern showed in her expression. "Are you? I'm sorry, I never planned on this happening, and I'm afraid Louis has already sent the woman Cass arranged for away. Perhaps we could call Marceline's and have them send her back."

"Louis?"

"My friend, Louis Benoit. You will like Louis. He thinks you're the finest actor in the Western Hemisphere."

"How nice. And is 'friend' a euphemism for pimp?"

"No, I can see you're still confused about all this. I am no *poule*. It was just a pretense so we could get to know each other." She smiled tentatively. "I didn't realize when I first came to this country how superstars like you are guarded. I tried everything I could think of to arrange a meeting. I wrote to your manager and to the publicity department, even to your private secretary. No one would even let me speak to you on the phone. The hotel reception desks won't even ring your room unless you tell them you're expecting a call. It was very discouraging." His expression remained both skeptical and suspicious, and Sacha sighed. "You're going to be difficult about this, aren't you?"

"Why not?" His brilliant blue eyes narrowed on

her face. "You told me you like difficult men." He turned, walked back to his chair, and sat down. "And I'm about to demonstrate just how difficult I can be."

"You're angry?"

"You're damn right. I don't like my privacy invaded. I don't like the idea of being a target for a confidence game and I don't like to be teased by a hooker who has no intention of delivering."

She studied him shrewdly. "I think it's the last that's bothering you the most. I told you I was sorry Louis has sent the blonde away." She came forward to stand before him. "But it's done now, and you must accept it. Forget about sex. We must talk."

"Forget about . . ." Indignation, outrage, and incredulity conflicted in his expression. Then, to her infinite relief, they were all superseded by amusement. "Maybe you're not a hooker after all. If you were, you'd know that sex isn't something that you can forget easily."

"Ah, now you're behaving sensibly." She smiled. "Of course, I'm not a hooker, nor a confidence woman. I'm your sister, and we're going to become great friends." She suddenly dropped to her knees before him and leaned back on her heels, gazing up at him earnestly. "That's all I want from you, Brody. I know you find it very hard to trust people these days, but you can trust me."

Her eyes were direct and without guile as they held his own. Brody studied her thoughtfully. My Lord, she actually believed what she was saying.

The realization brought a shock as profound as the initial announcement she had made. "And how do you know I have trouble trusting anyone?"

"Oh, I know all about you." Her expression was grave. "I've been studying you very carefully for the past two months. I suppose it's natural that you have to surround yourself with guards and walls, but it's sad too. Take Disney World, for example. You would have enjoyed that so—"

"Two months?"

She nodded. "That's when Louis and I came here from Paris. When I realized I wouldn't be able to see you by the usual means, I decided I'd have to find another way to do it. So I've been following you from city to city and getting to know all about you."

He leaned back in his chair, his face unreadable. "How interesting. You must be a determined young lady."

She nodded. "Very determined."

"And just what do you think you know about me?"

"Do you mean the surface things?" A tiny frown wrinkled her brow. "Well, of course, everyone knows you're a great actor. Your mother was Elise Merton, a bit actress who died when you were eleven. Your father and mine, Raymond Devlin, was also an actor. You spent most of your childhood in private boarding schools in London and Switzerland. You're not married, but have had many affairs." She paused. "But most of those happened when you were in your twenties. Lately you prefer to patronize very expensive call-girl services like Marceline's when you want a woman."

"I may think twice about that from now on," he murmured. "It seems to involve unexpected hazards."

She grinned. "Me? I'm no hazard. You'll see, I'll be very good for you."

A faint smile hovered on his lips. "Oh, you will, will you?"

"Yes, that was another reason I studied you so carefully. I want to be able to help you." She moved nearer, her face flushed with eagerness. "I've never had anyone of my own before, but I've always been very good with people. I'm sure I can be a wonderful sister to you."

Lord, the intensity she was generating was both mesmerizing and poignant. "You're planning on making that your full-time occupation?"

"No, that won't be possible. I have no money, and I have to—" She broke off as she caught the slight stiffening in Brody's demeanor and then shook her head sadly. "Don't pull away from me. I'm not going to ask you for money. I would never take anything from you. I just want to know what it's like to belong to someone, to belong to you. Family. I've wanted that since I was a little girl."

"Look, I'm not your brother," Brody said gently. "My father may have been a womanizer, but he wasn't a bastard who would have ignored the existence of his child."

"But he didn't know," Sacha said. Her fingers rose to rub absently at a spot behind her left ear.

"My mother was a gypsy singer in a cafe in Budapest. Raymond Devlin was there with a touring company for only a month and then returned to America. When she found she was pregnant, she was afraid to tell her father she was to have a *gajo*'s child. She would have been in disgrace with her tribe, and my grandfather hated *gajos*. She refused to tell anyone who my father was." She moistened her lips. "But she died when I was seven and left a letter telling me the truth."

"She named my father?"

Sacha shook her head. "She was still afraid my grandfather would hurt him. She only said he was a wonderful American actor."

"That covers a hell of a lot of territory."

"Not so much. There were only a handful of American actors in Budapest during that month."

His gaze narrowed on her face. "How do you know?"

"I had a friend check the immigration records."

"Evidently a very influential friend," he said softly. "I imagine it would be quite difficult to obtain that information after all these years."

Her gaze slid away from him. "He had certain . . . contacts." She made an impatient gesture with her hand. "But that's not important. Raymond Devlin was in Budapest during that month."

"And why did you single him out?"

"I saw a picture of the two of you together in a newspaper."

"And?"

"I have his eyes," she said simply. "Your eyes, Brody."

All trace of amusement vanished from Brody's face. He felt as if he'd been slammed in the stomach. The eyes looking into his own were undeniably similar to the ones he saw in the mirror every day, the same shade of blue, the same upward tilt at the corners. He had a fleeting memory of the impression when he had first seen her of something familiar about those eyes. Lord, could it be true?

His rejection came immediately and with violence. No, she couldn't be any relation; he wouldn't have it. His response to her had been too erotic, too powerful. Hell, his body was still aroused. Surely there was some instinct that would signal forbidden territory. "It could be coincidence."

"You don't really think that, do you?" Her face fell with disappointment. "No, it's the only answer. You must get used to the idea. I know it will be an adjustment, but I'll try to help. You'll soon forget that there was ever a time you didn't have a sister."

"And what if I don't choose to acknowledge the need for a sister?"

Pain flickered for a moment in her face, and then her lips firmed determinedly. "Then I'll just have to show you that you do need me. I've waited too long to find my family to give up easily. You needn't worry. I am not going to ask anything, but to let me give to you." She smiled tremulously. "I'm very good at giving."

He felt a tightness in his throat. If this was a con game, she must be the best in the business. "And in some circles I'm known as a world-class expert at taking. You'd better remember that."

Her face was suddenly illuminated by eagerness. "You believe me, don't you? It's going to be all right. You're going to let me—"

Two fingers were suddenly on her lips, silencing her. "Easy. I believe you think you're my sister, but that doesn't mean I necessarily do." Her lips felt warm and soft beneath the pads of his fingers, and he began to experience a tingling sensation spreading to his wrist and then up his arm. He hurriedly jerked his hand away from her mouth. "In fact, I doubt it seriously. We'll have to see."

She nodded quickly. "I won't rush you." Her eyes were shining. "I'll be very patient with you."

He chuckled. "You make me sound like a reluctant virgin."

"Bah, I would never make that mistake. I know too much about you." She stood up. "Now, I must go. I've given you enough to think about. Would you like me to call Marceline's before I leave?"

He thought about it. There was no question that he needed a woman but he suddenly found the thought of one of Marceline's girls unappetizing. "Maybe I'll do it later. Just how did you find out I used Marceline's service?"

"We asked questions. Louis was able to get a job as an usher in your theater in Dallas. You'd be surprised about the private details the stage crews know about you."

His lips thinned. "You're mistaken. It doesn't surprise me at all. My personal life has been fair game since I was a boy."

She nodded sympathetically. "I know that bothers you but—"

"You don't know anything about me," he said with sudden violence. "I wish you'd stop saying you do, dammit. You can't learn about a man by watching him act in a damn play."

"No?" She smiled. "If you say so, Brody. Then I'll be able to look forward to getting to know you now, won't I?"

He gazed at her helplessly. Why did he feel as if he were talking to the wind? "Where are you staying?"

She made a face. "The Majestic Hotel. Believe me, there's nothing majestic about it, but it's very cheap. Louis says it's a fleatrap but we needed to save every penny."

"Ah, yes, Louis." He stood up. "I'm anxious to meet your friend. Why don't you bring him around tomorrow afternoon?"

"We can't," she said over her shoulder as she moved toward the door leading to the sitting room. "We both have to work during the day. We'll see you tomorrow night after the performance if you'll leave word at the stage door to let us in."

He found himself trailing her into the sitting room. She was shrugging into her blue-jean jacket, and he suddenly became aware of how worn and faded the garment appeared. "How are you getting to the hotel?"

"Walking. It's only seven blocks."

"It's after midnight. Take a cab."

A glowing smile curved her lips. "You're worrying about me? That's a good sign."

"I'd worry about any woman on the streets at this hour."

"I'll be fine," she assured him cheerfully. "I can take care of myself. I'm very tough."

"You're not going to take a cab?"

She only smiled and turned toward the door.

"Wait." He strode to the telephone across the room. "I'll call for my car."

She smiled delightedly. "That will be nice. I've never ridden in a limousine. It will certainly up my stock at the Majestic. They may even try to raise my rent."

He found himself smiling indulgently as he spoke into the receiver. The girl was completely without affectation. He hung up the receiver. "Harris will be down in front of the hotel in five minutes."

"Harris?" Sacha repeated, rolling the texture of the name on her tongue. "He sounds wonderfully English and P. G. Wodehouse."

"He's from Brooklyn," Brody said dryly. "And he hates being away from New York with a very verbose passion. There's nothing stiff upper lip about him."

Her laughter pealed out, and he found himself tilting his head to listen. Husky and musical and full of earthy enjoyment. Lord, what a beautiful sound, Brody thought.

"That's even better," she said as she crossed to the door. "Good night, Brody."

"Wait," he said once more. He was experiencing a strange reluctance to let her leave him that had nothing to do with sexual desire. "You haven't told me anything about yourself. Don't you think that's a little unfair, considering you claim to know practically everything about me?"

She paused, her hand on the knob of the door. "There's not much to know. I told you my mother died when I was seven."

"And you grew up in Paris. With your grandfather?"

"No." She didn't turn around. "My grandfather never left Hungary."

"Then who did . . .?"

She opened the door hurriedly. "It's not important. What does it matter? I'm here now." She shot him a brilliant smile over her shoulder. "I'll see you tomorrow, Brody."

"Sacha, why . . .?" He trailed off. The door had shut behind her. He gazed at the carved panels thoughtfully for a few minutes before he picked up the receiver again and punched in Cass's room number.

The phone was picked up at once, as he knew it would be. Cass was an insomniac and seldom managed to get more than a few hours sleep a night. "Hello."

"Brody. Look, Cass, I want you to find out everything you can about a Sacha Lorion, age twenty-one, born in Budapest."

Cass's voice was instantly alert. "How do you spell her last name?"

"I'm not sure, but she's staying at the Majestic Hotel here in town. Probably with a man called Louis Benoit. They arrived from Paris two months ago. She's supposedly Hungarian and American. I don't know about Benoit."

"That's not much to go on." Cass paused. "Just how in-depth do you want this report?"

"To the bottom of the well," Brody said. "Everything."

"The best man to contact will probably be Randal, who handles your security. I'll call him right now, but this may take time."

"Grease the wheels. I want to know right away."

There was a short silence on the other end of the line. "May I ask what the hurry is?"

Brody's lips curved in a wry smile. He wondered what Cass would say if he told him he admitted to being a libertine but wanted the assurance that he wasn't an incestuous one. "The woman says she's my sister."

Cass gave a long low whistle. "A con game."

Brody scowled. "I didn't say that."

"You think there might be something to it?" Cass asked. "Raymond—"

"No, I don't think there's anything to it," Brody interrupted harshly. "Just check it out, okay?"

Cass hesitated. "Sure. Okay. I just thought—"

"Good night, Cass." Brody put down the receiver and turned toward the bedroom.

He doubted he would sleep. His body was still as aroused as the moment when he had held Sacha between his legs in the kitchen, and his mind was filled with guilt, bafflement, and the memory of Sacha Lorion's glowing face as she had looked up at him and said she wanted to belong to him.

"It went well?" Louis raised himself on one elbow and gazed at her sleepily. "He believed you?"

"Well, he didn't disbelieve me." Sacha grinned as she pulled her T-shirt over her head, then started for the bathroom. "I guess I couldn't expect anything more. It's going to be all right, you just wait and see."

Louis shook his head ruefully as she vanished into the bathroom. Sacha always thought everything was going to turn out fine, and most of the time it miraculously did. No, miracles had nothing to do with it. Sacha was the catalyst, the one who snatched success from the fires of failure.

Sacha came out of the bathroom in the orange oversize rugby jersey shirt in which she usually slept. She turned out the light and padded across the faded flowered carpet to the bed. The springs sagged as she slipped into her side of the double bed, plumped up the thin pillow, and drew the sheet about her shoulders.

She gazed into the darkness. She should try to

get some sleep. Tomorrow would be as strenuous as any other workday. She squirmed restlessly on the lumpy mattress. But how could she sleep when everything had changed? She had met him. They had talked and even laughed together.

He had *liked* her. Her hands clenched on the sheet, excitement rising within her. She knew he liked her even if he didn't yet realize it himself. Before that idiotic misunderstanding there had been moments when she had sensed a—a togetherness, a wonderful bonding of spirit like nothing she had ever known before. She had never realized that a blood tie could be this dynamic. After all these years she had someone of her own.

Louis's hesitant voice came out of the darkness. "Sacha, don't care so much. It may not work out."

"It will," Sacha whispered. "It's got to work."

"He's a hard man."

"Yes."

"You said yourself he didn't care about anything but his work."

"Yes."

"Did you tell him about yourself? He might not understand."

"I'm not ashamed of my past, Louis."

"I know that, but—"

"I'll tell him. I just didn't want to throw too many things at him at once."

"Sacha, maybe you should—"

"Oh, Louis, please be still. I'm so happy. Don't spoil it."

Louis was silent a moment. "All right, I won't

say anything more." There was another silence before he said fiercely, "But don't get too attached to this fine brother of yours. If he hurts you, I'll cut the bastard's heart out."

"It's going to be fine. You'll like him, Louis."

"Maybe. But I'll still cut his heart out."

Sacha laughed softly. "Good night, Louis."

"Bonne nuit."

He was asleep a few minutes later, but Sacha was still wide-awake, excitement bubbling within her. Everything Louis had said about Brody was true, but none of it mattered. He belonged to her. She could work out anything as long as that truth remained.

"This is my friend Louis Benoit," Sacha said. "My brother, Brody, Louis."

Louis Benoit was the most beautiful human being Brody had ever seen. He judged the man to be in his early twenties, with classic features, crystal-gray eyes, and a shock of dark hair that curled around that Greek-god face with stylishly careless abandon. Tall and slim, dressed in jeans and a black jacket, he possessed the easy grace of a top male model.

Brody nodded. "Benoit." The Frenchman was gazing at him with antipathy, and Brody found himself bristling with answering antagonism. His hand closed on the knob of his dressing room door. "I have to change. If you'll wait for me, I'd like both of you to be my guests at dinner."

"We'll wait," Sacha said happily. "Do you mind if we look around? I've never been backstage before."

"Go ahead." Brody found his gaze clinging to her eager face and forced himself to look away. "Be back in fifteen minutes."

Benoit started to turn away and then stopped. "You were very good tonight. You always are."

Brody experienced a flicker of surprise. "Thank you."

"You don't have to thank me. I merely tell the truth." Benoit turned and walked away.

Sacha made a comical face and whispered, "Sometimes Louis can be difficult too."

His lips twisted. "But worthwhile?"

She nodded. "Very worthwhile. Give him a chance." She hurried down the hall after Benoit.

Well, Brody didn't like him at the moment. He found the Frenchman surly, rude, and entirely too good-looking. He opened the door to find Cass sitting in the easy chair with his feet propped up on the coffee table.

His manager looked up from the papers he was scanning with an inquiring gaze. "How did it go?"

"Fine." Brody closed the door behind him and strode over to the dressing table. "Sacha Lorion and Louis Benoit are here."

"I know, the stage manager brought them to me and asked me to keep them out of everyone's way when they showed up backstage. Nice kids."

"I found Benoit a little grim."

Cass looked surprised. "Did you? I thought he

seemed like a great guy. He's fantastic-looking too." His eyes narrowed thoughtfully. "How do you think he'd photograph?"

"Looking for another client, Cass?" Brody asked dryly.

"A manager never has too many clients."

Brody began to take off his makeup. "I thought he was a little too pretty."

"Evidently his roommate doesn't agree with you."

Brody's hand hesitated for a tenth of a second and then continued to apply cold cream to his face. "Roommate?"

Cass gestured to the paper in his hand. "Sacha Lorion and Benoit share a room at the Majestic."

Brody found his hand clenching on a tissue and forced himself to release it. "That's the report?"

Cass nodded. "It was delivered by special messenger during the second act. It's fairly conclusive regarding activities since she arrived in the U.S., but we're having trouble finding out anything about her life in France." He shook his head. "I don't know what the holdup is, but Randal says they'll keep working on it. He was surprised that it was easier to find out about her life before she came to Paris." He paused. "She's not your sister, Brody."

Brody felt a rush of relief that was surely out of all proportion to the statement. "You're sure?"

"Your father was in Hungary at that time, but he was living with a ballerina by the name of Elena Woezak." He glanced down at the report. "He was at a small hunting lodge outside the city during the entire period the girl had to have been conceived."

"Then she's no relation at all?"

"I didn't say that. We're pretty sure she's David Brownlett's daughter. That would make her your fourth cousin."

"David Brownlett? I never heard of him."

"A distant cousin of Raymond's. He toured in the same show and was in Budapest during that identical period. All the preliminary investigation links him with the girl's mother. We should get final confirmation in a few days."

"I see," Brody said slowly. "Where is this Brownlett now?"

"Dead."

"Did he have any family?"

Cass shook his head. "None. Why?"

"No reason." That meant Sacha was still alone. The thought sent a poignant pang of regret through him as he remembered her face as she looked up at him and told him how much she wanted someone of her own.

"Do you want me to break the news to her?" Cass asked.

"What?" Brody's thoughts were still on Sacha and he forced his mind back to the present. "No, I'll tell her."

"It would be kind to do it soon so they can get on with their lives. They've been living hand to mouth for the last two months, while they've been following you around. They've got to be able to find better jobs than the ones they have now."

Brody's eyes met Cass's in the mirror. "What do you mean? What are they doing?"

"The girl is washing dishes and busing tables in a hash house down the street from the Majestic, and Benoit's delivering packages for a department store." Cass's glance returned to the report. "They've had similar jobs in every town since they began following you from city to city. They evidently had to take what they could get on short notice."

"Evidently."

"So tell the girl right away, okay?"

Brody nodded slowly. "Do me a favor? Take Benoit out to dinner and send Sacha in to see me."

Cass unwound his long legs and stood up. "Sure. No problem."

The door shut behind him.

No problem. Brody's lips curved in an ironic smile. Very simple. Just tell Sacha she belonged to no one. Maybe he could even offer her an exchange. How about trading a long-lost brother for a one-night stand? She should jump at a great deal like that. Hell, it was an offer he'd probably make her before the evening was over, if he ran true to form.

He muttered a low curse as he stood up and pushed the chair back from the dressing table. Dammit, he didn't want to feel sorry for the girl. He wanted to take off her clothes, pull her into the shower, and . . . He closed his eyes, feeling the arousal flood him as it had last night as he'd lain in bed, remembering that velvety skin and the clean, sweet smell of her.

His eyes flicked open, and he moved toward the bathroom, a faint reckless smile curving his lips. Well, why not? She was no child, and he sure as hell was no saint. Why shouldn't he take what he wanted as he had always done before? According to Cass, Sacha was practically destitute, and it wasn't as if he were planning on victimizing her. He would take care of her while she was with him, then give her a generous amount of money when the time came for—

Settlement. Protection. So it was to be no one-night stand after all. The realization came as no real surprise. He must have been planning this on some deep level since the first moment he had realized he wanted Sacha Lorion. Even then he had known that once would not be enough.

Three

"For Pete's sake, get out of there!" Cass Radison jerked open the shower door and reached in to turn off the spray. "I think your long-lost 'sister' is going to be turned into mincemeat in another two minutes."

"What the hell are you talking about?" Brody stepped from the shower and accepted the towel Cass handed him. "What's happening?"

"I'm surprised you didn't hear it." Cass tossed him his white terry-cloth robe. "The stagehands are laying bets who's going to knock out whom. Naomi is the odds-on favorite at the moment."

Brody jerked on his robe and hurriedly tied the belt. "Sacha and Naomi are *fighting*?"

"What else could I have been trying to tell you?" Cass asked impatiently. "And we can't break it up. Come and see if that damn little tiger cat will listen to you." He ran his fingers through his thinning hair, leaving strands sticking up like graying stalks in a winter wheatfield. "Naomi is going to kill her."

Brody raced from the bathroom and through the dressing room. He heard shouts and laughter the moment he reached the hall. Both sounds were issuing from a crowd at the far end of the corridor. He ran down the hall, pushing through the little circle until he came to the nucleus of the disturbance. Naomi, still in her nun's costume from the last scene, and Sacha were entangled on the floor. Even as he watched, Sacha lifted her knee in a wicked blow to the soprano's midsection. Then she flipped Naomi over on her back and leapt astride the larger woman.

Sacha's hair was no longer sleek but a wild aureole around her flushed face. A triangular tear marred her white cotton blouse and the pocket of her jeans had been ripped off entirely. Her eyes blazed fiercely as she gazed down into Naomi's furious face. "You will not do it again, you understand? Never again."

"Bitch," Naomi spit back.

"Perhaps." Sacha's hand tangled in Naomi's blond hair and pulled hard. "But if you are in the mood to slap someone, you'll call me and not vent your anger on a child."

"I'll do what I choose," Naomi said venomously. "You can't do this to me."

"I can do whatever I want—" Sacha broke off as Brody's arms encircled her waist and unceremoniously jerked her off Naomi's prone body. "No, you don't understand; it's not finished."

"Oh, yes, it is," Brody said grimly. "That amazon is almost half again your weight."

"I am not!" Naomi struggled to a sitting position, glaring at both of them. "Does this—this juvenile delinquent belong to you, Brody?"

"In a manner of speaking." Brody's voice was curt as he tried to subdue Sacha's wriggling body.

Naomi's expression took on added malice as she struggled to her feet. "Good, then I'll be even happier to tear her hair out."

"I told you it wasn't finished," Sacha said. "You heard her. If you stop us now, I'll have to do this all over again."

"Cass, get Naomi into her dressing room and don't let her out until she calms down," Brody ordered. His gaze fell on Louis Benoit, leaning lazily against the wall, a faint smile curving his well-shaped lips. "Why the devil are you just standing there watching all this? She's supposed to be your 'friend,' blast you. Do you like seeing her get hurt?"

Benoit shrugged. "Sacha knows what she is doing. She wouldn't thank me for interfering." His gaze went to Naomi. "And I've seen her take on far tougher opponents than this woman."

"You just think she has," Naomi hissed. "I'll get back at her and the boy too. You just wait. I'll show—" The vicious threat was abruptly cut off as Cass jerked her into her dressing room and slammed the door.

"Let me loose," Sacha cried. "Brody, this is none of your business."

"You've made yourself my business. I didn't ask to be referee in a catfight. Now stop struggling, dammit." He cast a glacier glance at the grinning circle of spectators surrounding them. "The show is over, break it up."

There was a sudden cessation of laughter, and the crowd immediately began to drift away.

Louis Benoit straightened and strolled toward a small towheaded boy dressed in the costume of a medieval peasant. He clapped the boy on the shoulder. "It was fun while it lasted, eh? What's your name?"

"Jimmy Marsden." The boy's freckled face lit with a mischievous smile. "Your friend's pretty good. Not that I couldn't have handled Naomi myself."

"Of course, you could." Louis's eyes were twinkling. "But it never hurts to have help, and Sacha's a good friend to have in your corner."

"Jimmy, stay away from her until I think of a way to resolve this," Sacha said urgently. "She'll be more vicious than ever until we convince her it will do her more harm than good. Brody stopped us much too soon."

"Too soon?" Brody was outraged. "She would have *murdered* you."

She stopped struggling. "You were worried about me? That's very sweet. I suppose I must forgive you for interfering."

"Forgive me?" Brody repeated. He counted to five. "I may decide to murder you myself."

"But the fault was not mine. Jimmy only played a small trick on Guenevere."

"Naomi," Brody corrected.

"Whatever. I've seen her so often as Guenevere that it's hard to think of her by any other name." She frowned. "How could such a horrible person act the part of a queen and make it believable? Anyway, Jimmy played a small trick on—"

"It wasn't that small," Jimmy interrupted indignantly. "I thought it was pretty cosmic."

"But not very original." Louis tilted his head consideringly. "A frog in her cold cream jar? It's been done many times before. And you should never have hidden in her dressing room to see her reaction. It would have been smarter to have come in with the crowd when she screamed and pretended complete innocence."

Jimmy grinned. "It was worth getting slugged to see her face when she opened the jar." He rubbed his cheek that was already showing a livid mark. "Though she's got a lot of power for a soprano." His admiring glance shifted to Sacha. "But you're even better. What a great left."

"Thank you." Sacha smiled. "And Louis is too critical. The frog in the cold cream jar is a classic. It can never be overdone."

Brody let Sacha slip from his arms but retained an iron grasp on her arm. "Do you suppose we could disperse this mutual admiration society?"

he asked caustically. "I'm still wet, and it's damn cold standing in this hallway."

"Oh, yes, of course," Sacha said quickly. "We'll go to your dressing room at once." She took a long look at him for the first time, her gaze encompassing his bare feet and legs, the wet hair plastered flat to his head, and the rivulet of water running down his cheek. "Good heavens, you could catch a terrible cold. How foolish of you to run out into this chilly hall with nothing on."

"Foolish?" He enunciated the word very slowly and with great precision. "I was rescuing you, dammit."

"Were you?" She gazed up at him, startled. Then her face lit with a glowing smile. "Oh, Brody, how wonderful. I'm sorry I scolded you. I don't think I've ever had anyone rescue me before."

Her expression was filled with such innocent delight that his indignation began to fade. A wry smile twisted his lips. "I can tell. You don't carry off the role very well."

Cass opened the door of Naomi's dressing room and dashed into the hall with the air of a man in flight. He hurriedly shut the door and leaned back against it with a sigh of relief. "I feel as if I've been through a tank attack."

"How is she?" Brody asked.

"Cursing, swearing vengeance, throwing things," Cass enumerated. "Shall I go on?"

"No." Brody turned away. "Suppose you take Louis and Jimmy out to dinner. I need to talk to Sacha."

"Fine," Cass said. "If they don't mind a restaurant with dim lights and soothing music. An old man like me needs to recuperate after facing a shrew like Naomi."

"Sacha?" Louis gazed at Sacha, waiting.

She nodded. "I'll see you back at the hotel." She turned to Jimmy. "Remember what I said. Stay away from her. I'll take care of it."

Jimmy nodded and waved, as Cass whisked both Louis and Jimmy toward the boy's dressing room.

"May we go now?" Brody asked politely.

"Yes, of course." Sacha linked her left arm through Brody's and strolled down the hall. "And I do thank you for your rescue. It was truly very—"

"Sweet," Brody finished for her. "I don't believe I've ever been called sweet before." He opened the door to his dressing room and motioned for her to precede him. "Nor have I ever attempted to rescue a woman before. It feels exceptionally odd."

"I'm sure it's wonderfully good for your character." Sacha entered the room, plopped down in the beige easy chair by the door and stretched out her jean-clad legs. "This feels good. I think I'm a little tired."

Brody suddenly found himself laughing helplessly. He closed the door and leaned against it, his face alight with mirth. "Amazing. You've just been through a knock-down-and-drag-out fight and you *think* you're a little tired. You're damn lucky you weren't hurt."

"I'm always lucky," she said lightly. "Now, get

dressed quickly. You mustn't catch cold or I'll feel most guilty."

"Heaven forbid." There was a lingering smile on his lips as he took his street clothes from the closet and disappeared into the bathroom.

He dressed quickly in jeans, sweatshirt, and loafers and ran a comb through his damp hair. He opened the bathroom door. "Was that quick enough? I'd hate to give you a guilt tri—"

Sacha's head was tilted back against the high rise of the chair, her eyes closed and her lips thinned in unmistakable pain. Her lids flew open, and she straightened hurriedly as soon as she heard his voice. She smiled. "That was very quick. You were most accommodating. Now, perhaps—"

"What's wrong?" Brody asked curtly.

"Nothing. I told you I was tired." Sacha struggled to her feet. "Let me tidy up a little and then I'll be ready to go."

"Don't lie to me." Brody crossed the room in three strides. "You're in some kind of pain. What's wrong with you?"

"I'm fine. I just need a little rest."

"Sacha, answer me," Brody ordered with dangerous softness. "We're not leaving here until you do."

Her gaze met his and she made a face. "You're being difficult again, Brody."

"Right."

"And you're not going to give up?"

"Right again."

She sighed. "I didn't think so." She held out her

arm. "It's my right wrist. Guenevere twisted it and—"

She was interrupted by a round of unprintable words as he saw her swollen and bruised forearm. "Why the hell didn't you tell me?"

"It isn't important. It will be fine once I get back to the hotel and bathe it. It's probably only a little sprain."

He took her right hand gently in both of his. "It could be broken," he said thickly. "Your bones are so damn delicate."

"No," she assured him. "I only look delicate. I'm actually very tough."

She had said that before, but there appeared to be nothing tough about either her or the hand he was holding. Both were slender and seemed infinitely fragile. "We'd better get you to the emergency room at the hospital and have them X-ray it."

"No!" She jerked her hand away. "No hospitals."

"Sacha, it would be better—"

"No! I don't like hospitals." She shook her head emphatically. "I won't go."

"But that's stupid. It will only take fifteen minutes or so, and then we'll be sure you're okay."

"I'm not going," Sacha said flatly. She turned away. "I'll go back to the hotel and bathe it. It will be fine."

"Hold it," he ordered curtly. "Very well, we'll let the X ray go for now. But if the swelling doesn't go down a hell of a lot by tomorrow, I'll drag you there by your hair. Now, sit down and let me see what I can manage in the way of first aid. I'll get a basin of water and a washcloth." He turned away. "I think I saw a kit in the medicine chest in the bathroom."

Ten minutes later Brody was still kneeling by the easy chair, bathing her wrist in cold water. He scowled intently as he transferred the cold cloth from the basin to her wrist for the umpteenth time. "I think it's going down a little."

Sacha nodded, her gaze fixed bemusedly on his face. "Oh, yes, it feels much better."

His gaze lifted from her wrist to her face. "Much? I thought you never lied."

"Well, I *do* exaggerate," she admitted with a grin. "But it's truly a good deal better, Brody."

"The hospital—"

"No hospital." Her smile faded. "I told you I don't like them."

"So you did." His frown deepened. "Idiotic. The entire episode is idiotic. You're idiotic. Why didn't you tell me right away you were hurt?"

"I thought the pain would disappear."

"And when you found it wouldn't?"

"I thought I could stand it."

"Why?" he asked explosively. "Why would you pretend not to be in pain?"

"I was afraid you'd send me away," she said simply. "I wanted to be with you, Brody."

He felt as if she'd hit him with a sledgehammer. Her expression was completely free of lies or armor, and he couldn't seem to tear his gaze away. "My God," he whispered.

"I love you," Sacha said softly. "I belong to you. I didn't want to let this silly injury interfere with your getting to know me."

He finally managed to look away from her. "You don't know what you're talking about."

"Yes, I do. I know *you*, Brody. It's you who doesn't realize what's happening. We've found each other. Can't you feel how important it is to both of us?"

"Sacha, there's something I have to tell you."

"What?"

"Cass received a . . ." His words trailed off as his glance returned to her face. Eagerness, radiance, happiness. How the hell could he destroy all that when she was also in physical pain? "Cass likes Chinese food, but I prefer Italian. How about you?"

"Anything." The radiance deepened. "You're not sending me back to the hotel?"

"We'll see." He opened the first-aid kit, took out an elastic bandage, and began winding it around her swollen wrist. "I'll take you out to a formal dinner tomorrow evening but perhaps we can go for a quick bite tonight before I take you back to your hotel. But you've got to promise to tell me if the pain gets worse."

She nodded. "I promise."

He pinned the bandage. "And let me comb your hair and wash your face. I refuse to be seen with a ragtag urchin like you." He took the damp wash-cloth and gently smoothed it over her flushed cheeks and forehead. "It's very bad for my image. Okay?"

"Okay." Her gaze was full of wonder. "I like this. I find it very . . . sweet."

He flinched. "That word again. Much more talk like that will really ruin my image." He took a small comb from his back pocket and began tidying her hair, which was as sleek and silky as it looked. The tresses flowed between his fingers, igniting a familiar tingling sensation. He hurriedly jerked the comb away and thrust it back into his pocket. He pulled her blue-jean jacket closed, covering her torn blouse. "That should do it. If the lights are dim, you might even pass for respectable." He stood up and pulled her to her feet. "Come on. Harris should be out in the alley with the car by now."

"I liked Harris," Sacha said. "I found him very—"

"Sweet?"

She thought about it as she preceded him from the room and down the hall. "No, that's not the word. No one who weighs nearly three hundred pounds and scowls a great deal could be called sweet. Interesting, I think."

"He smiles more in New York. In fact, that's the only place he does smile." Brody opened the heavy stage door leading to the alley. "I don't know why he insists on coming on these tours with me."

"Don't you?" Sacha smiled as she stepped out into the alley. "I think he cares very much for you. He would probably miss you if you left him behind in—"

"Hold it!"

A flashbulb went off, the brilliant light blinding

Sacha, making it impossible to see the man behind the camera. "Thanks, Mr. Devlin." Then the shadowy figure was gone, running down the alley toward the street.

Brody muttered a low imprecation.

"Who was it?" Sacha's voice was tense.

"I couldn't see. I've still got spots in front of my eyes."

"Do you think it was a newspaper reporter?"

"Maybe. Or it could have been just a fan. Everyone is a photographer these days." He took her arm and found she was trembling. "You're shaking. Are you cold?"

"No," she whispered. "You're right. It didn't have to have been a newspaper man. It could have been anyone."

He frowned, puzzled. "Sure. Is there anything wrong?"

She hesitated, then shook her head. "No, nothing's wrong. I guess I'm hungry, that's all."

Brody chuckled. "Brawling obviously whets your appetite." He urged her toward the beige Lincoln Continental parked a few yards away. "But please refrain from any further fisticuffs with Naomi. Like Cass, I believe I'm getting too old for this kind of thing."

"I promise there won't be any more brawls." Sacha's mind was obviously on something else. "But it's not finished."

"Sacha . . ."

She looked at him, her eyes grave. "She struck that boy. I have to make sure she never hurts a child again. Children are too easy for adults to victimize."

"Jimmy has an agent, a manager, and a very pushy stage mother to protect him. He doesn't need you."

"None of whom were there tonight."

"And he has me, Sacha," Brody said quietly. "Do you think I'd let that bitch hit Jimmy again?"

"No." She hesitated. "But it's still my responsibility. I promised him."

"Sacha, you can't—"

"Don't worry." She smiled. "I won't do anything violent. I promised you, remember? I'll have to think of something else." Her smile faded and her eyes narrowed pensively. "Yes, I'll have to think about it."

Naomi was gazing straight ahead, her demeanor suitably tragic as her hands were tied behind her at the stake by the soldiers of Camelot. The words of "Guenevere" resounded rhythmically from the chorus, and Brody Devlin was center stage in the throes of agonizing over the decision to burn his beloved.

Now was the time, Sacha thought. The stage was milling with soldiers and knights, and Brody, as usual, was holding the audience enthralled. No one would notice anyone but him while he was speaking. She slipped on stage, dressed in the steel armor and helmet of a medieval soldier, her hand holding the flaming torch steady as she drifted toward the stake from the rear.

Naomi caught a glimpse of movement from the corner of her eye, then felt the loose ropes looped and then tightened about her wrists. "What . . ."

"It's only me." Sacha moved to stand beside the stake, looking straight ahead and at attention. "I told you it wasn't finished."

The soprano stared in disbelief at Sacha. "What is this, some kind of masquerade?" she hissed furiously. "Loosen these ropes. Lancelot will be here any moment to rescue me."

"Then he may have a difficult time of it. I knotted the ropes, and none of those play swords are sharp enough to cut butter. In fact, you may even appear ridiculous." Sacha paused. "I've been wondering whether I should save you from that fate. Surely it would be better for an actress to be tragic than foolish." She lowered the torch toward the wood piled high around the stake. "It's very tempting."

"Are you crazy?" Naomi's eyes widened with fear. "I'll *scream*."

"They'd only think you were overacting, trying to steal the scene. I've noticed you do that quite frequently." Sacha lowered the torch another few inches. "Just one spark and—poof."

Naomi moistened her lips nervously. "For heaven's sake, it was only a little slap, and the brat deserved it."

"Are you feeling helpless?" Sacha asked mockingly. "It's not very nice, is it? Children are helpless too. They can be manipulated and victimized just like you at this moment."

"You're not going to do it. It would be insane."

"Are you frightened?"

"Yes!"

"Good, then maybe you'll remember how it feels. Because if I ever hear of you striking a child again, I'll be back. I'll find a way of getting to you just like I did tonight. There are worse things than a frog in your cold cream jar. How would you like a rattlesnake in your shower stall?"

"You wouldn't do that!"

"You'll never be sure, will you? The only thing you can count on is that I'll find a way of punishing you." Sacha stepped behind the stake and cut the ropes. "Yes, you can definitely count on that."

The music was rising, and Lancelot was fighting his way toward the stake. Sacha faded quickly off the stage and into the wings. She didn't have much time to get back to the wardrobe room and change out of her costume before she met Brody in his dressing room. She took off the helmet, shook out her hair, and turned to take one last look at Naomi. The actress was gazing at her with anger, outrage, and fear, but it was fear that was paramount. It was the response Sacha had striven to attain. Fear would keep Naomi firmly under control and Jimmy safe from abuse.

Sacha lifted her hand in a mocking salute. *Now* it was finished.

When Brody walked into his dressing room fifteen minutes later, Sacha was sitting in the easy chair reading a copy of *Variety* she had found on the coffee table.

"You know, I thought I understood English very well, but this paper is practically unintelligible to me. I suppose it's because it's some kind of trade jargon." She looked up with an innocent smile. "You're late. You must have had more curtain calls than usual. I'm not surprised. From the glimpse I caught from the wings, you outdid yourself."

"Well, someone outdid themselves," Brody said dryly. "I've just spent ten minutes trying to calm down a near-hysterical Guenevere. She barely made it through the last scene."

"Really?" Sacha looked down at the paper again. "Well, it was probably no loss. That was your scene anyway."

"She kept muttering something about human bonfires and rattlesnakes in shower stalls." Brody sat down at the dressing table and gazed at her suspiciously. "I don't suppose you'd know anything about that?"

"Should I?"

"Sacha, I want the truth."

She looked up with a glowing smile. "The truth is that Jimmy won't have any more problems with a very unpleasant lady." She held up her bandaged arm. "And that my wrist is very much better. It bothered me only a little at work today."

"You went to work today?" Brody asked with a frown. "Why the devil did you do a crazy thing like that?"

"Having my wrist in dishwater all day was therapeutic," Sacha said soothingly. "If I'd gone to that hospital you were trying to force on me, they'd probably have told me it was just the right medicine."

"I'd doubt if they'd—" He broke off and shook his head ruefully. "You lay a very tempting red herring. I take it you're not going to talk about Naomi's hysterical state?"

"It's over." Sacha threw the copy of *Variety* on the table. "Why talk about unpleasant things?" She stood up and turned in a circle. "Look at me."

She was dressed very much the same as she had been the other times he'd seen her, in blue jeans, a white T-shirt and a blue-jean jacket. "What am I looking at?"

"I washed my own face and combed my hair."

"Amazing. Another red herring?"

She laughed. "Just a little one." Her smile faded. "I'm sorry I don't have anything pretty to wear to dinner. Usually I don't care, but I would have liked to look nice tonight."

He frowned. "You look fine. I was joking when I gave you all that crap about my image last night. I thought you knew that."

"I did." Her eyes were suddenly twinkling. "You don't think I was apologizing to you? I'm sorry for me. I'm very vain and I like to look pretty."

He chuckled. "You do look pretty." She looked more than pretty, he thought. She was sparkling, shimmering, glittering with vitality. The impulse to reach out and touch her was a raw hunger within him. He didn't know how much longer he could keep his hands off her. He would have to tell her tonight. He looked away. "Where's Benoit?"

"He'll be here soon. He wanted to watch the performance. I told you he loved your work."

"And you wanted him out of the line of fire," Brody guessed shrewdly. "It seems that Jimmy isn't the only one who arouses your protective impulses."

"It's natural to protect the ones you care about."

"Is it? I'm afraid I've never been subject to that particular emotion."

"No?" She smiled gently. "And yet you've been protective of me, Brody."

"I haven't—" He stopped. "That's because you're so blasted stupid about taking care of yourself. You don't think, dammit."

"I always think . . . sooner or later. I just don't let it get in the way of my instincts."

"That's a very dangerous philosophy."

"But it works," Sacha said softly. "It brought me to you."

"Which should be a warning in itself. Sacha, I want—"

There was an urgent knock on the door before it opened and Louis Benoit walked in. He completely ignored Brody as he turned to Sacha. "I think you should see this." He tossed her the folded newspaper in his hand. "It's the evening paper. I got it in the machine outside the theater." He shut the door behind him, watching Sacha's face as she glanced at the captioned picture.

She inhaled sharply. "Oh, damn, he *was* a reporter."

Brody stood up and crossed the room to stand beside Sacha. The picture was very clear, and Sacha's features were quite beautifully defined as she stood in the stage doorway beside Brody. "You photograph very well," he said casually. "It must be those great cheekbones. Have you ever done any modeling?"

"Yes, once." Sacha's gaze had not left the picture. One finger lifted absently to rub a spot behind her left ear. "They don't have my name. Will this be carried overseas?"

"If the AP picks it up."

"And they probably will," Louis said quietly. "Devlin is big news."

"I think they will too," she whispered. "Oh, *damn!*"

"What's wrong?" Brody asked, his gaze narrowed on her face. "You're white as a sheet. Look, I'm sorry you're upset about being seen with me. I know it can't do your reputation any good, but it's not that big a deal. No one will remember this photograph next week."

The newspaper slowly crumpled as her hand clenched on it with white knuckled force. "I have to leave. Blast it, I didn't want this to happen now. Not now." Her eyes were glittering with tears. "It was all going so well."

Brody took a half step closer. "Look, tell me what's bothering you. It can't be all that bad. Let me help you."

"You can't. It's my problem." She turned suddenly, threw herself into Brody's arms, and hugged him with desperate strength. "I can't stay. Oh, Brody, don't forget me. Please don't rally all your guards around you to keep me away from you when it's safe for me to come back."

"Safe?" A chill trickled down Brody's spine. "Why shouldn't you be safe now?"

Sacha stepped back, and her arms fell away from him. "Good-bye," she whispered. Then she was gone, dashing through the door held open by Louis and disappearing down the hall.

Brody took a half step forward but was stopped by Benoit's hand on his arm. "No," the Frenchman said quietly. "Let her go. You'll only be a danger to her."

"Danger? What the hell is going on?" Brody's gaze searched Benoit's face. "And why should I make the situation any worse? It's clear she's scared to death."

"A spotlight follows you around." Benoit shrugged. "Sacha can't afford to share that spotlight right now. Let her alone."

"With you?" Brody asked fiercely. "You don't like to share her with anyone, do you?"

A flicker of surprise crossed Benoit's face. "You think we are lovers?" His eyes narrowed on Brody. "I wonder why it should matter to you if we are? I find your attitude curiously unbrotherly. You might almost be . . . jealous."

Brody muttered a low curse and threw off Benoit's grasp. "I gather you know why she's so frightened?"

Benoit nodded. "But I'm not telling you. That's Sacha's right to tell or not." He turned to the door. "But I can say that the consequences could be very serious if you persist in enlarging the spotlight on you to include Sacha."

"How serious?"

Benoit looked back over his shoulder as he once more opened the door. "You could get her killed."

Four

Brody's first knock on the hotel-room door went unanswered. He knocked again. No response. "Sacha, dammit, let me in. I know you're in there. I checked downstairs at the desk."

The door was immediately thrown open. Sacha stood there, her cheeks flushed, her dark hair ruffled. "You shouldn't be here, Brody. I told you—"

"Nobody has told me anything that makes any sense." Brody pushed open the door and stepped into the room.

Louis Benoit, sitting on the bed beside an open suitcase, gave him an unsmiling nod. "You don't listen very well. Stay away from her, Devlin."

Brody slammed the door behind him. "The hell I will." He turned to Sacha. "Now, tell me who you're running away from. The police?"

Sacha shook her head. "We've done nothing against the law. It's something else entirely."

"What?"

"I can't tell you. Not now. I won't involve you in my problems." Sacha crossed to the bureau and drew out the remainder of the clothing in the top drawer. She crossed the room and placed the pile of garments in the open suitcase. "Louis is right. It would be better if I stayed away from you. I would never forgive myself if you were hurt."

"So you're just going to disappear and leave me wondering what's happened to you?" Brody strode across the room, slammed shut the suitcase, and fastened the metal latches. "Sorry, but I'll be damned if I'll let you get away with that. I don't like to worry, and you'd have me a basket case before the week was out."

Sacha became still. "Why, Brody?"

"I told you I was a very sensitive fellow." Then he looked up to meet her gaze. "I don't know. Anyone will tell you it isn't at all like me to become involved in something that's obviously going to be a big headache, if not actually lethal. I'm too selfish to ask for trouble." He suddenly smiled with surprising gentleness. "I guess I want to help you. Benoit seems to think that being with me would give you away to whoever is after you, but it could also offer you protection. You said yourself I was surrounded by guards wherever I went, and I'll order security doubled immediately. Maybe we can even catch whoever is after you. Isn't that a better plan than running away and hiding in the shadows? You can stay with me at the Ventura until the show closes two nights from now, and then I'll take you to my home at Malibu."

Sacha shook her head. "It's asking too much of you."

Louis said thoughtfully, "He's right, Sacha. It might be a way to end it."

"And risk his life doing so," she said fiercely. "No, I wouldn't ask anyone to do that for me. How could I ever repay it?"

"I'm not asking you to repay me," Brody said impatiently. "I'm just asking you to be sensible."

"But I would have to repay you." Sacha's voice was passionate with intensity. "You don't understand. Not paying a debt is like stealing." She smiled shakily. "I suppose you don't know me well enough yet to realize I can't bear to be in debt to anyone."

She meant every word she was saying, Brody thought. In another moment she'd walk out that door and he'd be helpless to stop her. His hands clenched slowly into fists at his sides. Helpless, hell. There was no way he was going to let her leave him. He forced himself to relax. "You've forgotten one thing. It's natural for the members of a family to help each other. No payment is expected between a man and his . . . sister."

Her eyes widened. "You *believe* me? You believe we're related?"

He nodded curtly. "I believe we're related." He grabbed the suitcase off the bed. "Now can we get the hell out of this dump?"

She hesitated. "I suppose it is all right." She

suddenly smiled brilliantly. "There are no debts between brothers and sisters. Only love, right?"

He gazed at her a long moment feeling his throat tighten. "No debts," he echoed thickly. He turned to Louis Benoit. "You're welcome to come along if this mysterious danger is leveled at you too."

Benoit shook his head. "I'm in no danger. It's Sacha that Gino's after."

"Gino?" Then, as Brody saw Sacha's expression become troubled, he held up his hand in resignation. "I know. You can't tell me. I believe I'm getting very tired of all this melodrama. I go through enough of these hijinks on stage to put up with it in my private life."

"I'm sorry," Sacha said. "But I have no right to burden you with—"

"That's enough. I've heard it all before," Brody growled. "You're not coming, Benoit?"

Louis stood up. "No, I think I'll stay here. I'll have the desk move me to another room and see if any visitors show up at the hotel looking for Sacha." He smiled at Sacha, his brown eyes warm. "Who knows? Maybe we're wrong. Maybe Gino won't come at all."

"Maybe." Sacha moistened her lips and absently rubbed her left ear. "But I doubt it. We both know how fond Gino is of making examples." Her hand fell to her side, and she turned to Brody. "But you must tell these guards they are to protect you first. You understand? Nothing must happen to you because you're helping me."

"Nothing is going to happen to either of us." He

took her elbow. "Can we leave now? This place is very depressing to my delicate sensibilities. If we must be in danger, let it be in a five-star hotel."

She chuckled. "By all means. I can see how you'd be upset. Louis and I are used to roughing it."

His gaze left her face to wander to the double bed. "You and Louis are obviously accustomed to doing a great many things together."

"We've been friends a long time." Sacha's answer was abstracted as she turned to Louis. "Don't take any foolish chances and don't let Gino see you."

Louis's lips twisted. "He probably wouldn't even remember me. I wasn't important to him." He added bitterly, "There were so many of us."

"Well, don't risk it." She turned to Brody and smiled. "See how I trust you? I'm placing myself entirely in your hands."

He nodded, his expression shuttered. "That's exactly what I had in mind, though not in precisely this fashion." He propelled her toward the door. "We'll just have to see how it works out."

"You can have the bed. I'll sleep on the couch in the sitting room." Brody motioned to the door of the bedroom. "Clear out any drawers you need in the bureau for your things."

She made a face, "One drawer should do it. I don't have much."

"Why not? I don't believe I've ever met a lady who could pack all her clothes in one suitcase."

Her gaze slid away from him. "I had a larger wardrobe in Paris. Not anything to rival Imelda Marcos, but adequate. I had to leave there in such a hurry that I ended up with just the clothes on my back. What I have in that suitcase are the things I've managed to buy since I've been here."

"Like Donald Duck?"

She grinned. "That T-shirt was an extravagance I couldn't resist. Wearing it makes me happy, and that's important too." Her smile faded. "I don't want your bed, Brody. I'll take the couch."

He shook his head. "I'd feel better if I slept in the sitting room. You've infected me with a strange malady that feels dangerously like gallantry. I've been experiencing the most unusual symptoms of wanting to guard and protect." He shuddered the-atrically. "I can't bear to anticipate what other virtues will emerge from this situation in which you've involved me."

"Bah! You're too set in your ways to be in any danger of total reformation." Sacha's blue eyes were dancing. "But a little will do you no harm." She turned to the bedroom. "All right, I'll let you guard me, but there's no sense you going to ex-tremes while you do it. That couch looks far too elegant to be comfortable. We'll both take the bed."

The smile faded from Brody's face. "We will?"

"Why not? It's much wider than the one Louis and I shared." She glanced back at him as she opened the door. "And I don't snore, I promise you. It would be stupid not to share."

Something flickered in Brody's face. "I certainly

wouldn't want to be thought stupid as well as gallant."

"Good. Then it's settled."

"Not quite."

She looked at him inquiringly.

"I sleep in the raw."

"Oh, that's no problem, so does Louis." She went into the bedroom, leaving the door open. "May I have the shower first?" she called back to him.

"Why not?" There was a thread of sarcasm in his silky tone. "Unless you'd prefer we shower together? Perhaps that's another activity you shared with Benoit, and I certainly wouldn't want you to get lonesome."

"Of course, we did not shower together," Sacha said, surprised. "There are some things a person prefers to do in private."

"Very few things, evidently," he muttered as he appeared in the doorway and leaned on the jamb, watching her.

Sacha opened her suitcase and took out her orange rugby jersey. "Well, one does like company for most activities. At least I always have. I suppose I'm naturally gregarious." She turned and moved toward the bathroom, feeling his gaze on her back as she opened the door. "I'll be right out."

Brody was behaving most peculiarly, she thought as she quickly stripped off her clothes and dropped them on the gleaming white tiles of the floor. Well, who could blame him? He had suddenly acquired a live-in sister, a possible threat of violence to himself, as well as total disruption of his privacy. It was no wonder the tension surrounding him was nearly tangible. Poor Brody.

And wonderful Brody. How lucky she was to belong to him. Behind that hard facade she had discovered gentleness, humor, and a surprising sweetness. She never would have dreamed that he would want to shoulder her problems like this. She shouldn't have let him. It was wrong of her, but dear heaven, she didn't want to leave him now that she had just found him.

She rummaged in the elegant white basket on the vanity and found complimentary bottles of shampoo and body lotion. She opened the small bottle of shampoo and sniffed ecstatically as she stepped into the shower stall. What a heavenly floral scent, Sacha thought. She would feel marvelously luxurious using it after the generic brand to which she was accustomed. Brody was right. If you had to be in danger, you might as well be comfortable.

After a long shower and shampoo she anointed her body with lotion and talc, feeling blissfully sybaritic. Then she slipped on her orange jersey and wrapped her wet hair in a towel.

"I'm sorry I was so long," she called as she gathered her discarded clothes together and opened the door. "I could become addicted to a bathroom like this. It's absolutely wonderful."

Brody was already in bed, she noticed, as she walked into the bedroom. He was propped up against the headboard, the satin sheet draped carelessly across his lower body. The triangular thatch of hair pelting his naked chest was the same rich chestnut shade as the hair on his head but was not as smooth and gleaming. It looked thick, wiry and tough. *He* looked tough. The muscles of his shoulders shone sleek and powerful in the golden circle of lamplight surrounding the bed.

Sacha stopped beside the bed. How odd. She was curiously breathless, almost shy, and there was a tingling in her palms as she gazed at the chestnut hair roughing Brody's chest. "Don't you want to shower?"

He shook his head. "I always shower after the performance." His smile was self-mocking. "Though I may feel the urge for a cold shower before morning."

Her brow wrinkled in a puzzled frown. "Does that happen very often?"

"Not since I was fourteen. Come to bed, Sacha."

"In just a minute. I need to dry my hair a little more." She set her clothes neatly on a maroon velvet wing chair, then sat down on her side of the bed and began to rub her hair briskly.

"There's a blow-dryer in the vanity cabinet."

"Is there? I never thought to look. It doesn't matter. My hair is very fine and dries quickly."

"It matters." Her head was enveloped in the towel, and she didn't see the tension that tautened the muscles of his abdomen as he watched the soft orange jersey mold and cling to her small breasts when she lifted her hands to rub her hair. "It matters a hell of a lot." His voice was hoarse. "Go get the dryer."

She lowered the towel, her dark hair a wild frame for her flushed, glowing face. "I'm sorry. You're right. I'm keeping you awake." She jumped up from the bed and ran into the bathroom. She found the dryer and came back to the bedroom. "Do you know where the outlet is?"

"There's one in the bathroom."

"I'd rather do it here. It's more companionable." She came around to his side of the bed and looked behind the nightstand. "Here's one." She plugged in the hair dryer and sat down on the floor. She crossed her legs tailor fashion, facing him, and turned on the hair dryer. "Talk to me."

He pulled his gaze away from the silken flesh of her naked thighs and forced himself to look at her face. "You have a thing about being companionable, don't you?"

She nodded, holding the nozzle of the dryer to the left side of her head and lifting the curls with her fingers. "Oh, yes, I think it's very important that we choose friends and become close to them. Otherwise it can be terribly lonely." She looked at him soberly. "I think you're very lonely, Brody."

"I wouldn't say loneliness was my problem. I have too many people around me most of the time."

"But no one you let close to you. That can be even worse than being alone." She switched the dryer to the opposite side of her head. "When I was a little girl, I was surrounded by other children, but sometimes I still felt isolated. I guess we all do. That's when I'd close my eyes and think about what it would be like to have a real family of my own."

"Other children? Were you in an orphanage?"

She hesitated. "Something like an orphanage." She suddenly scooted close to the bed and turned around so that her face was hidden from him. "Will you dry the back of my hair for me? It's always the hardest to reach."

He didn't answer for a moment. "Hand me the dryer." He swung his feet to the floor on each side of her as he reached for the dryer.

She closed her eyes in purely sensual pleasure as the soft warm air caressed her nape and Brody's fingers combed through the damp tresses. His naked legs were cradling her between them. Brody really had beautiful legs, she thought dreamily. She had known they were well shaped; the tights of his costumes outlined every muscle of his calves and thighs, but bare, they looked far more virile and brawny. His feet, planted on the deep blue carpet, were strong and shapely, and the tanned thighs on each side of her were dusted with fine, sun-lightened hair.

"Are you asleep?" Brody asked.

"No, I was just thinking what nice feet you have." She leaned the side of her head on his thigh, letting the warm flow of air weave through her hair. His skin felt deliciously rough against her flesh, and she rubbed her cheek back and forth with catlike pleasure, enjoying the textures of him.

"Stop!" Brody's voice was suddenly charged with tension, the muscle beneath her cheek clenched and rigid.

She chuckled. "Am I tickling you?"

"You could say that." His voice was guttural. He turned off the dryer and put it on the bedside table. "I think that's enough." His legs were gone from around her as he pulled them back, scooted up, and slid under the sheet. "Hell, I know it's enough. Turn out that light and come to bed."

Doubtfully she touched her hair. It still felt a little damp to her, but Brody was obviously impatient. She scrambled to her knees and reached over to turn out the lamp. In the darkness she padded around the bed and slipped beneath the satin coverlet. The springs were firm, the mattress comfortable, and the satin sheets cool and slick. Magic. Positively magic.

"What's wrong?"

"Nothing. Why?"

"That sigh almost shook the bed."

"Contentment. No lumps. Do you know what a luxury a mattress with no lumps can be?"

There was a pause before Brody said slowly, "I guess I'd forgotten. The last time I even thought about comfort was in Vietnam. I was nineteen and I remember how cold and hard the ground was. And the rain. . . ." There was a silence then. "I thought I'd never forget that hell. I guess I didn't really forget. I just blocked it out."

"We all block things out. It helps us to survive and go on. But you're so lucky, Brody. You have

everything you need to make a wonderful life."
She hesitated. "You could be happy if you let
yourself."

"I'm perfectly content. Why shouldn't I be?"

"Bah, content is for beds that aren't lumpy. Happy
is different. Happy is . . ." She searched wildly for
words. "Oh, I don't know. Rockets going off and
flags waving and a shining inside. You don't have
that, Brody, and I want it for you."

"Do you?" His voice was husky. "Thank you,
Sacha, but you'll find my 'shining' is a little
tarnished with wear, and I launched most of my
rockets a long time ago."

"You sound like an old man. It's a good thing I
got to you when I did." Sacha chuckled. "Stick
with me, and we'll find you brand-new rockets to
send soaring."

Lord, he felt jaded. There was nothing tarnished
about the shining within Sacha. She glowed with
a clear inner beauty that moved him profoundly.
"I believe I may do that."

There was a long silence before Sacha spoke
again. "Being in bed with you is different from
being in bed with Louis. He's more . . . comfortable."

"And I'm not?"

"No." She sounded puzzled. "You're so tense
that I think you're making me a little tense too. I
feel . . . odd."

"I suppose I'm not accustomed to sleeping with
anyone." He added silkily, "Of course, you don't
have that excuse."

"I guess that must be it." She paused. "But you're always tense, aren't you? I used to watch you on stage, and I could almost feel it. There were times when it was worse than others, but it was always there. Why?"

"Go to sleep." His tone was suddenly abrupt. "I'm not in the mood to bare my soul tonight. Why should I confide in you, when you won't tell me a damn thing about yourself?"

"No reason," she said. "I guess I just want to know everything about you."

"Well, you've found out enough for one night. Go to sleep."

"I know I'm a chatterbox. Does it bother you?"

The flow of words didn't bother him so much as her voice—soft, husky, stroking him in the darkness. He had thought once the light was out and he couldn't see her, it would be easier. He had been wrong. The darkness enhanced the sensuality of the sensations he was experiencing. With every breath he took in the warm, floral scent clinging to her skin and hair. And that voice . . .

Would he ever be able to sleep? He was aching, throbbing, the blood tingling through his veins, surging into his groin. What an idiot he was being to let her do this to him. Why didn't he just *tell* her, and then reach out and bring her to him? She was warm and responsive, and he was an experienced lover. He could *make* her respond.

But he didn't want to make her respond. He wanted her to come to him and offer herself. He wanted to treat her with gentleness, show her beauty, and know he hadn't tarnished the wonderful shining within her. And if he did tell her, what if she left him and ran headlong into the dangerous situation Benoit said might kill her? How the hell had he gotten himself into this mess?

He heard her resigned sigh as she turned over and made herself more comfortable. A short time later her breathing altered, steadied, and he knew she was asleep.

He didn't move for another five minutes, waiting for her slumber to deepen. Then he slipped from the bed, shrugged into his robe, and padded to the door leading to the sitting room. A minute later he was at the desk punching in Cass's room number on the phone. Cass picked up the phone on the second ring. "Cass, I need you to contact Randal right away."

Cass chuckled. "It's three-thirty in the morning. Lord, Brody, you must be becoming an insomniac too. Not that I'm complaining, you understand. The worst thing about not sleeping is the loneliness. Why do I have to contact Randal? He'll give me the report as soon as he gets it."

"I want my security doubled and expanded to cover Sacha Lorion."

Cass was no longer laughing. "You're expecting trouble?"

"Possibly."

"From whom?"

"I haven't the slightest idea," Brody said. "Just take care of beefing up the security. It seems that Sacha has a past that may become very actively present. I'm keeping her with me at all times both here at the suite and at the theater."

"Oh." There was a pause. "How . . . interesting."

"Cass . . ." Brody stopped. How could he clarify the situation to Cass when he didn't understand it himself? "Oh, never mind. Good night, Cass."

"I wish," Cass said wistfully. "If you can't go back to sleep, why don't you come down the hall and we'll play a hand or two of gin rummy?"

Brody hung up the receiver and strode back to the bedroom. He moved silently to the bed and untied the belt of his robe. He had a press conference at ten and he might as well try to get a few hours sleep even if—

The *scent* of her—floral, evocative, wafting to him in the darkness. His heart began to pound. Heat flooded his loins.

"Damn!" He turned on his heel and strode out of the bedroom and across the sitting room.

His hand was trembling as he reached for the phone. "Cass, I can't leave Sacha alone here, but why don't you bring that gin rummy game down to my suite?"

Five

"Where to tonight?" Brody asked as he took Sacha's elbow and propelled her down the hall toward the stage door. "I hear San Diego has some fabulous Mexican restaurants."

"We could go to an all-night grocery store and shop for food. Then I could make a meal for us at the suite," Sacha suggested. "I didn't really get an opportunity to show you what a wonderful cook I am. Quiche is no challenge."

"I don't think that would be a very good idea." Brody didn't look at her as he opened the door and allowed her to precede him. "I wouldn't want to impose. It's late, and you must be tired."

"Why? All I've done today is trail around after you to press interviews and previews and meetings. It's you who should be tired." She frowned disapprovingly. "You should not have stayed up all night playing cards with Cass. Do you do that often?"

"No, not often."

"Then, it *is* me," she said despondently. "You could not sleep with me. You should have told me. You said you weren't accustomed to sleeping with anyone but I thought— Tonight I will sleep on the couch."

"Neither one of us will take the couch. I called housekeeping and told them to send up a rolla-way bed and put it in the sitting room."

"I am being a great bother." She cast him a worried glance. "Perhaps I should not let you do all this for—"

"Hello, Barry." Brody smiled at the thin sandy-haired man waiting outside the stage door. "Everything okay?"

The young man nodded. "No sign of trouble, Mr. Devlin."

"Sacha, this is Barry Levine from Randal Security."

"How do you do," Sacha said. "Have you been standing out here all evening just waiting for us?"

Levine looked surprised. "Well . . . yes, ma'am."

A flicker of concern crossed Sacha's face before she smiled brightly. "I've always wanted to meet a private investigator. You must do a great many more interesting things than wait in alleys for people like Brody and me. Why don't you come to dinner with us and tell us all about your job? I think Brody wants Mexican food. Perhaps you don't like it?"

The young man looked slightly dazed. "I love Mexican food but— "

"Fine. Then it's settled, you will join us for dinner. Do you have your own car or will you go with us? Harris is parked over there." She gestured at the Lincoln and then turned to Brody. "Do you suppose Harris would like to join us too? It must be very lonely for him just sitting in the car."

Brody's lips were twitching. "We can only ask."

"My partner and I have our own car," Barry Levine said. "But I really don't think—"

"Then you will follow us, and tell your partner he must come too." Sacha started toward the Lincoln parked a few yards down the alley. "We will see you at the restaurant. I will tell Harris to go slow so that you can follow us and not get lost."

"Mr. Devlin . . ." Levine looked at him helplessly.

Brody nodded solemnly. "Yes, Barry, be sure you don't get lost." He fell into step with Sacha, feeling Levine's bewildered gaze on them as they walked down the alley. He suddenly began to chuckle.

"Why are you laughing?" Sacha asked.

"I was thinking about what Randal is going to say when he hears that his man had dinner with the client. He prides himself on his men's discreet, self-effacing image."

"This Randal sounds very stuffy. Why shouldn't that poor young man have dinner with us?"

"Poor?"

"Well, can't you imagine how depressed he must get just standing around waiting for something bad to happen? And look how thin he is. I'm sure he doesn't eat properly. We must make sure he has a good meal tonight, at least."

"By all means. Now let's see, tonight we take care of Harris's boredom and Levine's nutrition problem. Do you think we should pick up the cop on the beat and see what we can do for him?"

"Stop laughing." Uncertain, she looked up at him. "You don't really mind, do you?"

His laughter faded but the warmth lingered in his eyes. "No, I don't mind," he said gently. "We may have an interesting evening." He opened the passenger door of the limousine for her. "I'm sure it won't be boring."

She got into the limousine and settled herself comfortably on the maroon velvet seat. "Then you invite Harris," she whispered. "I think he would like it better."

He nodded. "Wait until we get to the restaurant. I don't want to rattle him while he's driving." He got into the car and shut the door. "Harris has an even greater sense of place than Randal." He leaned forward. "Mexican, Harris."

The red-haired driver nodded. "Right, Mr. Devlin. There's a restaurant two blocks away that's supposed to be pretty good." He put the car in gear, cruising slowly down the alley toward the brightly lit street. "As good as anything can be in California. The people out here don't know how to do much of anything." The long limousine emerged from the alley, and Harris stopped, waiting for an opportunity to turn into traffic. "Remember that

Mexican restaurant on Broadway? Way uptown? Now, *that* was a good— *Damn* what . . .!"

The glass of the window next to Sacha exploded and then shattered. She froze, staring at the small hole in the glass.

"Get down!" Brody shouted. He hurled himself across the seat, covering her body with his own. The glass shattered again and there was a sickeningly solid thunk. Brody's body stiffened against her.

A bullet! That had been a bullet, she thought in panic. Someone was shooting at her, and Brody had— She could hear Harris cursing, she felt the sudden cool rush of air as the door beside her was jerked open. Something warm was flowing down her breast. Blood! Had she been shot?

"Are you both all right?" It was Levine's voice. "It was a sniper from the hotel across the street. My partner's on his trail right now and— Merciful God!"

"Is it safe to leave her?" Brody asked tersely. "Damn you, Barry, this wasn't suppose to happen. What the hell is the use of having security if you can't even keep one woman safe?"

"You're shot," Levine said, dazed. "God, I'm sorry, Mr. Devlin. We never expected a sniper. I'll call an ambulance."

It was Brody who was shot! "Get off me," Sacha whispered. "Brody, why did—"

He looked down at her. "Are you hurt?"

She nodded. "No, but you are. Oh, Brody." Tears

stung her eyes, and she couldn't seem to get more words past the tightness of her throat.

"I'm okay." He moved off her and collapsed on the seat beside her. His face was pale and taut as he leaned his head back and closed his eyes. Blood. Blood on the sleeve of his white shirt, blood dripping down his arm. "Harris, take me to the nearest emergency room."

"I'll call an ambulance." Levine started to turn away. "It shouldn't take long for them to get here. There's a hospital about eight blocks away."

"No!" Brody said sharply, opening his eyes. "That nut may still be around. We're not staying here. Follow us to the hospital and see if you can manage to prevent Sacha from getting murdered on the way." Then, when Levine continued to stand there undecided, he shouted "Get going, dammit!"

Levine stepped back and slammed the door. "The hospital is on the next street over. Take a left at the corner and then head north."

Harris started the car and stomped on the accelerator, skidding recklessly out into the traffic. "Just hold on," he said huskily over his shoulder. "I'll get you to that hospital double quick, Mr. Devlin."

Sacha moved across the seat. "The blood," she said numbly. "I've got to stop the blood. Where were you shot?"

"Only in the left arm."

"Only," she echoed. What if he was dying? What if the bullet had severed an artery and he was bleeding to death? The thought jarred her out of the chill of horror that had paralyzed her. "I don't have anything to cut your sleeve away but you need a pressure bandage or a tourniquet or something. Harris, do you— "

Harris tossed her a white cotton towel. "I use this to clean the windows. Don't put it on the wound, but it might do as a tourniquet."

She swiftly tied the towel tightly around Brody's arm above the source of blood on his sleeve. "Hurry, Harris, please hurry."

"It should be the next block," he said. "It will only be a few minutes."

She anxiously studied the primitive tourniquet. Oh, Lord, why couldn't she remember more about first aid? You were supposed to loosen tourniquets, but she couldn't remember how many minutes before they began to endanger the circulation. "Harris, do you know how—"

"Here we are." The limousine turned onto the hospital emergency lot and up to a ramp leading to a double door. Harris jumped out and came around to open her door. "If you want to run in and get some help, I'll stay with him."

She didn't want to leave Brody. He hadn't moved since they had started the journey and she didn't know whether he was unconscious or not. What if he died before she came back? If she was here, she would find a way to pull him back and keep him with her. He *belonged* to her. She refused to let death have him. "You go." Her arms slid around Brody, holding him with fierce possession. "I'll stay with him."

Harris nodded and whirled toward the emergency room. "Keep an eye on that bleeding."

He barreled through the doorway, throwing the double doors wide, and disappeared into the hospital.

"How is he?" Cass Radison's voice was jerky as he strode into the emergency waiting room.

Cass's gray hair was rumpled, and his face was almost as pale as Brody's had been before he had been taken away from her, Sacha realized. "I don't know, they wouldn't let me stay with him while they examined him. They took him into one of those rooms." She gestured to a wide black door across the room. "I told them he needed me, but they wouldn't let me go with him."

"Are you okay?" Cass's eyes narrowed on her taut face and then traveled to the bloodstains on her white T-shirt. "Harris said no one had been hurt but Brody."

"I'm fine. It's Brody's blood." She shuddered. Brody's blood. Brody's life in danger. "He saved my life, you know. It's my fault he was shot."

"Forget it. That's water under the bridge," Cass said impatiently. "Right now we have to worry about making sure Brody will be fine. *Damn* those security men."

"I owe him my life. I can't forget it." She folded her arms across her breasts, hugging herself, trying to stop the chill. "What if he dies, Cass?"

"He won't die. Harris said he didn't think it was serious. It was only an arm wound."

"Only!" Her eyes were blazing. "That's what Brody said. What's wrong with all of you? He was *bleeding.* What if—"

The black door suddenly opened and a short stocky man dressed in blue-green cotton trousers and tunic strode into the room. "Miss Lorion?"

"Here." Sacha hurried forward. "How is he? He wasn't hurt badly?"

"I'm Dr. Farland. Mr. Devlin will be fine; the bullet only grazed his arm."

Relief surged through her with dizzying strength. "Thank God," she murmured. "I was so afraid—"

"Can we take him back to the hotel?" Cass interrupted. "This place is going to be swarming with reporters and police as soon as word gets out. Brody isn't going to feel like answering questions."

Dr. Farland shook his head. "We'd like to keep him overnight to make sure he doesn't go into shock. We gave him a shot when we first began working on him, and he's still pretty groggy." His lips twisted. "We don't like the idea of the media crawling all over here either, but the hospital has no desire to be accused of negligence in Mr. Devlin's case. The best we can do is arrange to put him in a private room on the VIP floor and instruct the head nurse not to permit any visitors. Some member of his family will have to sign the admittance forms."

Sacha aroused herself from the euphoria of relief. "I'll sign them. I'm his sister."

The doctor frowned. "I've never read anything about Mr. Devlin having a sister. I'm afraid we'll have to ask for some form of proof."

"I don't have any proof, but I'm truly—"

"She's not his sister." Cass's words cut through her protest. "But I have his power of attorney. Will that do?"

Sacha stared at him in bewilderment. "But I *am* his sister. I can sign!"

Cass shook his head regretfully. "Look, I'm sorry, Sacha, but we have proof that you're no close relation whatsoever." He turned back to the doctor. "There's been a little misunderstanding here. Will the power of attorney be sufficient?"

"I don't see why not. See the admittance clerk and sign the papers." He sighed wearily. "And I'll try to keep everyone away from him but necessary staff. I hate it when we get celebrities here." He turned and strode down the hall.

"I don't understand," Sacha spoke very slowly, trying to pierce the gray mist of confusion and shock surrounding her. "You *know* I'm not Brody's sister?"

He nodded, his eyes sympathetic. "We received a report two days ago and a confirmation this morning. You're the daughter of David Brownlett, a fifth cousin of Raymond Devlin's, who was in Budapest at the same time as Brody's father."

"David Brownlett," Sacha repeated, her expression blank. "Yes, I remember that name being on my list." She was silent a moment, trying to comprehend it. Brody was not her brother. He did not belong to her. "Why didn't Brody tell me?"

"I'm sure he meant to." Cass shrugged. "David Brownlett was dead and had no remaining family. Brody probably found it difficult to break the news to you."

"You mean, he felt sorry for me," she whispered. "And when he found out I was in trouble, he was too kind to tell me."

"Kind?" Cass raised a brow. "I don't believe I've ever heard Brody referred to as kind."

"He is kind," Sacha said. "You don't understand him. He can be—" She broke off and closed her eyes. She drew a deep, quivering breath. "But he shouldn't have been kind this time. He shouldn't have let me impose on him." She laughed huskily, and her lids opened to reveal blue eyes glittering with tears. "*Impose* is such a weak word, isn't it? He saved my life, and I'm *nothing* to him. How can I ever repay him? How can I . . . ?" She trailed off helplessly.

"Sacha, he's not going to want you to repay him," Cass said quietly. "Whatever his reason for helping you, it wasn't to make you indebted to him. He doesn't play that kind of a game."

"But the debt exists, and I pay my debts." She ran her fingers distractedly through her hair. "I'll have to find a way of paying this one too. I don't know. I'll have to think about it."

"Let me take you back to the hotel," Cass said.

"You can't do any more here, and Brody would want to make sure you're safe."

"Did they catch the man who shot Brody?"

Cass shook his head. "He was gone by the time the security man located the hotel room the shot came from." He paused. "Do you know who he was?"

"Not exactly. It could have been either Gino or one of his friends."

"Gino?"

"Gino Amanti. He wants to kill me," she said flatly. "I don't want to talk about this now. It would do no good. You won't find him. Gino is too clever at evading the police. The only way I can make sure Brody is safe is to keep away from him. I shouldn't have let him talk me into staying with him, but he seemed so sure his security could protect us." And she hadn't wanted to leave him. She had wanted to stay with Brody and she had almost cost him his life. "It was a mistake."

"Let's go back to the hotel," Cass repeated. "You look as if you're ready to pass out at any second."

A faint smile touched her lips. "You're a very nice man, Cass. I do not deserve your kindness. I almost killed Brody."

"Bull," Cass said roughly. "I don't know what this is all about, but you're not the type of kid who would do anything wrong. Brody is a grown man, and he knew what he was doing."

"I hope so. I don't think I could bear—" She stopped abruptly. "I'm not going back to the hotel. I'm staying here with Brody."

"Sacha, you can't help—"

"I'm staying," she interrupted. "I want to be with him. Can you arrange for them to let me stay in his room, or shall I spend the night here in the waiting room?"

"There'll be reporters all over the place. They'll eat you alive if they find you out here."

"Then you'd do well to make sure I'm stowed away safely in Brody's room, now, wouldn't you?"

Cass sighed. "I guess I'd better. Wait here, I'll go sign those papers and see what I can do."

Dawn streaked the sky with mauve and palest gold. Through the open blinds at the window the warm colors of sunrise poured into the room, bathing Brody's body. His face, even though gray and drawn because of the gunshot wound, was still mesmerizing, Sacha thought tiredly. Spellbinder.

It seemed like such a long time since that night she had sat in the audience and tried to pinpoint Brody's appeal. He was no longer only the spellbinder; he was real to her. He was a man who could laugh at himself and the world around him, a man who could be gently and caring, a man who belonged to her.

But he didn't belong to her. It was hard to remember that Brody was not her brother when she still felt so close to him. If she walked out that door right now, she knew she would still remember the sound of his laughter—and the way his eyes could soften from hardness to tenderness in the space of a heartbeat—for the rest of her life. How could he not belong to her when she still felt like this?

Brody's lids quivered and then slowly opened, his gaze focusing on her face. "Sacha?"

Sacha's hands closed tightly on the arms of the visitor's chair. She had been expecting, waiting, for this moment all night, but it still came as a shock. "Good morning. May I get you anything? Shall I call the nurse?"

"No." He gazed at her drowsily. "What are you doing here?"

She shrugged. "I thought you might want company. Hospitals are not warm, wonderful places."

"I remember you saying you didn't like them. Have you been sitting in that chair all night?"

"Why not? It was better than sitting in the hotel and worrying. I wouldn't have slept anyway."

"There was no need to worry. The doctor says I'm going to be fine."

"Yes." She moistened her lips. "They didn't catch the man who shot you. Cass said to tell you that Randal is still working on it. The police are going to want to see you too. He says he'll try to stall them until you leave the hospital."

"Ah, yes, the police." His gaze narrowed on her face. "What am I going to tell them, Sacha?"

"What you like." She looked at the tranquil blue and green of the seascape on the wall across the room. "It doesn't matter."

"They'll want to talk to you too," he said softly.

"And they'll know by now that the shot was meant for you, and I just got in the way."

"You saved my life." Her voice was muffled. "You could have died."

"Oh, for Pete's sake, I received a worse wound than this doing one of my own stunts in my last film," he said. "What did you expect me to do? Sit there and let them take potshots at you?"

"No, you wouldn't do that." She paused. "And, if it happened again, you would probably do the same thing. That's why I have to leave. I only stayed to say good-bye."

"Don't talk nonsense. If you thought you were in danger before, you can be sure you are now. It would be damn stupid to run away from the protection my security men can offer."

Her lips twisted. "Would it be better to put myself in a position where you might have to throw yourself in front of me again? No, thank you, Brody. I owe you too much already."

"You don't owe me anything. I thought we agreed that there weren't any debts where—"

"Stop it!" Her tone vibrated with pain. "No more lies. I'm nothing to you."

He went still. "Cass told you."

"It was necessary. The hospital admittance . . ." Her gaze left the picture to fasten on his face. "Why didn't you tell me? Why did you let me think I had someone of my own?"

"I tried, dammit." Brody's expression was troubled. "One thing seemed to lead to another and every time I tried, I ran into a wall."

"Oh, I know." She made a jerky motion with one hand. "You felt sorry for me. You wanted to help me. You should not have done it. It . . . hurts, Brody."

"I never meant to hurt you."

She was silent for a moment, struggling for control. "It was not your fault. I'm wrong to blame you." She stood up. "Thank you for being so kind to me. Please forgive me for all the trouble I've brought you."

"Sit back down," Brody growled. "You're not going anywhere. I don't see why you're so upset. So you're not my sister. We're still related, and that should give me some right to take care of you."

"A sixth cousin?" She slowly shook her head. "That's no relation at all."

He smiled suddenly with the wheedling charm that had dazzled audiences for the last decade. "How can you say that? You have my eyes."

She started to laugh, and her voice suddenly broke. "Oh, Brody."

"Come with me," he said coaxingly. "Let me send you to Malibu, where you'll be safe. I'll have Randal surround the place with an army of guards so thick, you'll stumble over them every time you go out on the deck. I have one last performance tonight, and then I'll join you." His voice lowered to a velvet murmur. "We'll sit on the beach, and you can help me decide whether I'm going to do that science-fiction film or try a new play on Broadway."

"It sounds wonderful," she said wistfully. "But I can't let you do it. You've been too kind already."

"Kind? Stop saying that!" His smile had vanished. "I wasn't kind at all. Do you know why I had Cass investigate your claim? I wanted to make sure you weren't my sister before I seduced you. I had a yen, and I wanted to satisfy it, like I've satisfied every desire I've ever known. I was a selfish bastard who was acting entirely in his own interests."

Her eyes widened. "You wanted to go to bed with me?"

His lips twisted. "If you know me as well as you claim, that shouldn't surprise you."

"I thought it was just a momentary whim." She gazed at him with childlike gravity. "Do you still want to go to bed with me?"

He started to shake his head and then stopped. "Yes. I won't lie to you. I probably want you more than any woman I've ever wanted in my life." He paused. "But don't let it worry you. I promise, if you come to Malibu, I won't lay a hand on you. For once in my life I'm trying to think of someone else first." His lips curved in a crooked smile. "Who knows? Maybe playing noble King Arthur for the past three months has given me some kind of subliminal conditioning. I always did try to live my roles."

"Don't joke," she whispered. "You're doing it again. Giving to me. Piling up the debt so high, it's going to smother me."

"Look, what can I say to you?" Brody's voice

was suddenly harsh. "You barge into my life, torment me, worry the hell out of me, and then you decide to run away and drive me crazy thinking you're dodging bullets all over the state of California. If you owe me anything, it's peace of mind. You're being selfish as the devil, you know."

"I am?" She frowned uncertainly. "Would you really worry that much, Brody?"

"You're damn right I would."

"I don't know what to do." Her index finger reached up to rub behind her left ear. "I'm so confused. I thought I knew what I should do and everything was clear, but now . . ."

"It is clear. You owe me. Cass takes you to Malibu this morning."

Sacha's gaze searched Brody's face a long moment. She suddenly sat down in the visitor's chair. "Very well."

Brody released the breath he hadn't realized he'd been holding. "Now you're being reasonable."

"I'm not sure about that, but the decision is made." She paused. "There are a few conditions. You must make sure this Malibu place is safe for you. I won't endanger you again. You must let me help you however I can. I won't be a burden." She met his gaze. "And you must never lie to me again, not even by omission. We must be honest with each other. Agreed?"

He nodded. "Agreed." He leaned back on the pillows and closed his eyes. He was silent for a long time, and she thought he had gone back to sleep. Then he suddenly began to chuckle.

"Something is funny?"

He didn't open his eyes, and his voice was faintly slurred. "I was just thinking, if Guenevere had made it this difficult to be rescued by Lancelot, she would have burned to a crisp before he managed to whisk her from the stake." He tried to smother a yawn. "You've got to learn to be . . . more accommodating. . . ." The words trailed off, and she knew he was asleep again.

Sacha slowly leaned back against the cushioned blue plastic of the chair, her gaze on Brody's face. "I'm going to try," Brody," she said softly. "Lord knows, I intend to try."

Six

"Come in, Brody. Why do you knock? After all, it's your house." Sacha hurried forward, smiling. "Did you bring the groceries?"

"Would I dare disobey your orders?" Brody asked lightly. "Harris is getting them out of the trunk of the car right this minute. The clerk at the all-night supermarket thought I was stocking a fall-out shelter. I think I got everything on the list, but we have enough food to feed a small army. Do you mind telling me why we need five cans of coffee?"

"For the security men," Sacha answered. "It *is* a small army. Do you realize there are seven men outside? Naturally we have to keep them in refreshments."

"There's no 'naturally' about it." Brody's lips tightened grimly. "Let's hope they're more efficient than they were that night outside the theater." He stepped aside to let Harris through the doorway. The chauffeur, burdened by three shopping bags, was followed into the house by Barry Levine and another security man similarly encumbered. The three men disappeared down the corridor in the direction of the kitchen. "You don't have to cook for Randal's men. They certainly won't expect it."

"I'll enjoy it," Sacha said. "It will give me something to do. Besides, I like to cook." She smiled at Harris and the other men as they came back to the foyer. "Thank you all very much. Remember, Barry, send a man to the kitchen for coffee at seven and ten tomorrow morning. We'll work out the rest of the schedule once I get organized."

"Right." Barry Levine nodded. "Whatever you say, Miss Lorion."

The door closed behind them.

Sacha's smile faded. "Now we can get down to what's important. How is your arm?"

"Fine. It's only a little stiff."

"You should have come here with me this morning and told them you couldn't do the show. Surely they wouldn't have expected you to go on when they knew you had just come out of the hospital."

"The house was sold out." He closed the front door and leaned back against it. "It was no problem. Actually it was more exhausting trying to explain the shooting to the police, but I think I've kept them off your trail for the next day or so at least." He grinned, his blue eyes twinkling. "Ham that I am, I kind of enjoyed all the fuss being made of me at the theater. It's not often an actor gets a chance to play such a juicy martyr role. Besides, I got terrific press. 'The show must go on' and all that rot."

"But it's not rot to you," she said softly. "You're not nearly as cynical as you pretend to be, Brody. You're actually a very dedicated man."

"Are you looking into your crystal ball again? I told you that you didn't know everything about me."

"No, but I'm learning more all the time." She turned and started down the foyer toward the kitchen. "Come along, I've already made your dinner. It's only a stew, but you're lucky to get anything at all. There was nothing in the refrigerator, and I had to send that nice Barry Levine to pick up the ingredients. That's why I called the theater and gave my grocery list to Cass. It's enough to have to worry about being shot without starving to death too."

A smile tugged at his lips. "Why do I feel that you prefer the bullets?"

"Well, it's true that I don't like to be hungry. Things always look brighter when your stomach is full." She gestured to the breakfast nook across the kitchen, where a place had been set and a steaming bowl of stew smelled mouth-wateringly delicious. "I dished it up when I heard the car outside. Sit down and eat while I put away the groceries."

"Aren't you going to have anything?"

"I ate earlier." She began to unpack one of the sacks on the counter. "But I'll stay and talk to you while you taste my wonderful stew. I know I never like to eat alone. It's much nicer to have someone to chat with." She glanced over her shoulder with a smile. "Not that I give you much chance to talk. Tell me to be quiet when you get bored with my chatter."

Brody raised his gaze from the contents of the bowl in front of him. "You never bore me." He smiled slowly with a warmth that made her catch her breath. "I like to hear you chatter. I find it very . . . companionable."

Sacha could feel the hot color surge to her cheeks. The reaction startled her, and she found herself gazing at Brody with a strange, breathless shyness. What was wrong with her? It wasn't like her to react with this lack of composure once she'd reached a decision. Yet there was no question that she was distraught. Even her hands were trembling as she finished unpacking the groceries. She turned around and tried to keep her tone light. "Are you making fun of me?"

"A little. Do you mind?"

"Why should I? I hope I don't take myself so seriously that I can't laugh at my own foibles." She opened the door of the refrigerator and began storing the milk and other perishables. "This is a fine house, very luxurious and expensive. Do you like it?"

"It's fine, I suppose. I bought it last year fully furnished, and I never thought much about it. It

was just a place to come to when I needed privacy
to work. I guess I liked the private beach more
than any other feature."

She breathed a sigh of relief. "Oh, good, then
you won't mind if I don't like your house. I was
afraid if I was honest I might hurt your feelings."
She opened the cabinet door and began shelving
the canned goods. "It's really a dreadful place. So
cold. It has no personality and that's the most
terrible thing a person can say about a house.
But don't worry. I'll find a way to make it livable."

"I'm sure you will."

"Do you like your stew?"

"It's magnificent."

"I knew you would love it. Wait until I cook my
beef Stroganoff for you. How did the performance
go tonight?"

"Okay, I guess."

"You sound tired." She glanced over her shoulder with quick concern. He looked as weary as he
sounded, she noticed with a rush of maternal
tenderness. "Finish eating quickly and go to bed."

"I couldn't sleep."

She turned around and studied him thoughtfully. "You're not only tired, you're very tense,"
she said slowly. "Why? The tour is over. I would
think you'd be able to relax now."

"Would you?" He took another bite of stew. "It
would be nice if all our reactions could fall into
nice little reasonable patterns."

"Don't be sarcastic with me. I want to help you."

"Then for God's sake, let—" He broke off as his
gaze rose to her face. He drew a deep breath.

"Look, I'm sorry. Maybe it would be better if you left me alone. I'm a moody bastard, and I can be pretty savage at times."

"But you don't like yourself when you're this way. I don't know why you want to be alone. It's always easier to bear a burden if you have someone else to share it."

"I'll be okay."

"Brody . . ." She gazed at him helplessly. The tension radiating from him was nearly painful in intensity, yet his expression held a stubbornness that filled her with exasperation as well as despair. She suddenly couldn't stand it any longer. She slammed the refrigerator door shut. "Dammit, Brody, this is stupid." She marched across the room toward him. "And I hate stupidity more than almost anything in the world. Particularly when it's hurting someone I care about. This has got to stop." She dropped to her knees beside him. "Now, *talk* to me."

His lips were twitching as he tried to smother a smile. "Do you have a violent aversion to chairs? You seem to be constantly on your knees in front of me."

She made a face. "Which should be very good for your ego." Her smile faded. "You're not going to distract me, you know. Now, tell me why you are like this. It has something to do with your work. Right?"

"Very perceptive of you."

"Not really. Your work is the only thing that's really important to you. I would be very stupid if I didn't connect the two."

"You make me sound completely one-dimensional."

"Oh no." Her eyes were glowing softly as she gazed up at him. "You have so many facets. You're like a wonderful kaleidoscope, changing with every movement to form new patterns, yet always returning to what you truly are. Right now something is blocking you, but we can fix that."

"Can we?" He looked down at her in bemusement.

She nodded. "Talk to me. That's all you have to do. We'll take care of it together."

"It's not that simple, Sacha."

"Yes, it is." She scooted a few inches closer and rested her arms on his knees. "Something went wrong tonight?"

"No more than usual."

"How many curtain calls?"

"Nine."

"Then you were a great success. What's the problem?"

"I wasn't a success," he burst out with barely leashed violence. "I'm terrible in this role. I can't sing and I ham up every soliloquy. All I have is presence, and a decent pair of legs in tights."

She started to laugh then stopped as she saw his face. He was perfectly sincere, and she had an idea the problem was more far-reaching than his few words indicated. "The critics don't seem to agree with you."

"Subjective. I know my own capabilities."

"Do you?" Her brow wrinkled in a thoughtful frown. "How did you feel about your performance in *Hamlet* last year?"

He laughed harshly. "Tolerable. At least I didn't have to make an ass of myself singing."

Only tolerable. Yet the critics and public had hailed him as the greatest Hamlet of the generation. "I see." She *was* beginning to understand. "Then you think you failed?"

"I always fail." His jaw tightened and his teeth clenched. "I try so damn hard, but it's never what it should be. I don't see why they can't see it. Someday . . ."

"Someday they'll find you out. The critics and the public will realize you're not what they thought. They'll know you fooled them."

He nodded.

She shook her head. "No, Brody. They'll never realize how you cheated them. Not in the next century."

"They will. I know—"

"Listen, Brody." Her hands closed on his knees, her expression intent. "What did you think of Peter O'Toole's performance in *Becket*?"

"Mesmerizing."

"And Delacroix's painting *Liberty Leading the People*?"

"Magnificent."

"And the way Shakespeare constructed *Macbeth*?"

"Sacha, what the hell has this to do with anything?" he asked impatiently.

"I'm trying to make a point. Don't you see? I bet if you asked O'Toole or Delacroix or Shakespeare, they would have said that they had failed too. It's the tragedy of the creators of this world that their final work of art *never* fulfills the vision of what they think it should be. That doesn't mean their accomplishment isn't great or special. Yes, you have presence. You're a real spellbinder, but you're more than that. You're a great actor. You give us all memories that we'll cherish forever. You may never be satisfied with what you give us, but that doesn't mean we won't be satisfied, Brody. We can't see your vision, so we don't know what we're missing. The beauty you reveal is enough for us." She added softly, "More than enough."

"Sacha—" His eyes were glittering in his tanned face as he reached out with one gentle finger to trace the high contour of her cheekbone. "I believe I'm . . . overwhelmed. I feel quite peculiar."

"You believe me?" she asked urgently. "It's most important that you know what you are. Then the tension will go away." She snapped her fingers. "Like that."

"Sounds easy." A faint smile curved his lips. "You almost convince me."

She studied him shrewdly. "But not entirely. I think this may be more difficult to accomplish than I had believed. You're a very bullheaded man, Brody."

"But I have decent legs in tights," he reminded her lightly. "I have it on the best authority."

She sighed. "I can see you're not going to talk about it anymore. Oh, well, I'll just have to keep working on it." She sat back on her heels. "But you're still tense. Is there anything that helps?"

He was silent for a long moment. "One thing." He met her gaze. "But it's not an option that's available to me at the moment."

Heat. A fluid melting. A breathless tingling. There was something in his eyes that caused sensations to cascade over her in a wild, jumbled flow. Her breasts felt strange, swollen, the nipples taut and engorged, ready. . . .

"Brody . . ." Her voice sounded faint and uncertain even to her own ears, and she couldn't seem to pull her gaze away from Brody's. "What . . . ?"

It was finally Brody who managed to look away. He pushed the half-empty bowl of stew impatiently aside. "Go to bed. I'll put the rest of the groceries in the cabinet."

"No, I'll—"

"I said, I'll do it." His tone was sharp. "Did Cass get you settled in the guest room?"

"Yes, I'm very comfortable." She slowly got to her feet and stood looking at him. "Brody, don't push me out. I want to help you."

"You did help me." He didn't look at her. "You fixed me a wonderful meal and listened to my self-pitying blather. Now that you've done your duty, you deserve a good night's rest." He stood up, strode over to the counter, and began to put away the remaining groceries. "Good night, Sacha."

She stood watching him uncertainly. His movements were jerky and uncoordinated and the line of his spine taut. It was clear she had been dismissed. It was also clear Brody was going to refuse to let her help him. Oh, dear, she thought, he was exhibiting quixotic and unreasonable male characteristics she had never been aware he possessed. Well, she would just have to act on her own initiative to overcome his resistance. She immediately felt more assured once her decision was made. "Good night." She started for the door. "Oh, one more thing, Brody." She glanced over her shoulder. "You know the authority who assured you your legs in tights were decent?"

He frowned in puzzlement. "Yes?"

"He was wrong." She winked with mock lasciviousness. "They're not decent, they're absolutely fantastic."

She heard him utter an amused chuckle as she strode out of the kitchen and down the hall toward the guest room.

Sacha turned out the light and ran swiftly across the bedroom. The silk sheets were cool against her naked flesh as she slipped into the wide bed. Too cool. Sleeping on silk had seemed wonderfully luxurious that night at the Ventura but now she longed for the comfortable familiarity of the textures to which she was accustomed. Silk was as foreign to her as this beautiful, cold house; as foreign as this wild situation into which she had been plunged.

The water abruptly cut off in the shower, and Sacha's grip unconsciously tightened on the sheet covering her. Her heart was pounding so hard, she could scarcely breathe. Stupid. She was being so stupid to be this nervous. She consciously forced herself to relax and took several long, steadying breaths.

The bathroom door opened and the light flicked out. She couldn't hear Brody's footsteps on the deep pile of the thick rug but she knew he was coming toward the bed. She could discern the solidness of his moving shadow among the darker shadows in the room. Then the shadow stopped short in the middle of the room. Brody stood still, painfully alert, as if sensing some unknown danger.

"Sacha?"

She drew a deep quivering breath. "How did you know I was here?"

"Your scent. . . . What the hell are you doing in my bed?"

"It's where I belong," she said simply. "You said you wanted me."

Brody muttered a low curse and was suddenly walking toward the bed again. She involuntarily tensed. He sounded furious, but surely that would pass when . . . She blinked as he turned on the light and instinctively made a motion to pull the sheet up to cover her naked breasts. Then she stopped and deliberately let her hands fall to the counterpane of the bed. She tried to smile. "I'm sorry but I suddenly feel shy. It's not at all like me. I'll be better soon."

"The hell you say," he said grimly. "Well, I don't think I will." He gazed swiftly around the room. "Where the devil is your robe?"

"I don't have one." She moistened her lips with her tongue. "But I wouldn't wear it, if I did. It's better that I become accustomed to being naked in front of you. Then I won't feel quite so awkward. I notice you appear to be very comfortable." Her gaze traveled over him admiringly. "You're even more stunning nude than clothed. I didn't realize you had such a truly fantastic tush and the muscles of your shoulders are—"

"Sacha," he said between clenched teeth. "Shut up!" He saw his own terry-cloth robe slung over the back of a chair, snatched it up, and tossed it to her. "Put this on."

She shook her head.

"Dammit." He strode across the room, grabbed the robe from the bed, and draped it around her shoulders. "Now, keep it on."

He smelled of soap and musk and something deliciously male. She could feel the furnacelike heat radiating from his body, and it warmed her, taking away the nervous chill. She impulsively leaned forward and pressed her lips to the warm smoothness of his shoulder.

He flinched away as if she had burned him. "Don't do that!" he said thickly. He backed away a few paces, gazing at her as warily as if she were a wild animal occupying his bed.

"Why not?" Her gaze flicked to his lower body. "It's clear you want me to touch you very much."

His gaze followed her own and he muttered a low imprecation.

She shrugged his robe from her shoulders and it fell to the bed behind her. "You see? You're not being at all reasonable. You want me and I'm here. It would be foolish not to make love to me. I know you generally prefer a different type of woman, but I seemed to attract you before. And then in the hospital you said—"

"Go back to your room, Sacha."

She shook her head. "You're breaking your promise. You said you would let me help you any way I could."

His gaze was fastened compulsively on the beautifully delicate swell of her naked breasts. His tongue unconsciously moistened his lower lip. "I was thinking about cooking and washing the dishes."

She smiled. "I wasn't."

Brody forced his gaze to move from her breasts to her face. "Dammit, I won't have you doing this for me. I feel like a white slaver. You don't want this."

"How do you know? I'm not sure myself. It's difficult to tell when I'm so nervous." She met his gaze. "But I do know that I want to give you whatever you need from me."

"Gratitude," he bit out.

She shook her head. "Debt."

"Well, you can take your debt and cram it," he said roughly. "You don't owe me a thing. I never do anything I don't want to do."

She sighed. Brody was being very difficult about this. She would obviously have to escalate matters at once. Unfortunately she wasn't sure exactly how to go about it. Well, when in doubt . . .

She threw aside the sheet and stood up.

"For heaven's sake, Sacha!"

She walked slowly toward him. "I want you to know it's not only the debt," she said earnestly. "I do care about you very much, Brody." Ah, that was better, she thought with satisfaction. There was a flush mantling his broad cheekbones, and his eyes were smoky with something both hot and urgent. "I might want to do this regardless."

"Might? How flattering," he said caustically.

She stopped before him, her gaze searching his face. "I'm being very clumsy. It's only because I'm so nervous. I didn't mean to hurt you."

"You didn't—" He broke off as she reached out and touched him. A great shudder ran through him and he closed his eyes.

"So smooth." Her hand tightened around him. "And warm. I always wondered—"

"Let . . . me . . . go. "

"All right." She released him, then stepped close until her breasts were pressed against the chestnut thatch of hair on his chest.

She gasped. The abrasiveness was wildly erotic. Her nipples burned, then hardened, engendering a strange hot ache between her thighs. "Oh, I like this."

His lids opened slowly, heavily. "You do?"

She nodded emphatically, rubbing against him with catlike sensuality. "Yes." She arched her head back and her eyes half closed until they were brilliant blue slits veiled by her dark lashes. "I feel an odd sort of hurting, but the pleasure makes up—"

The words were smothered as his lips covered

her own with hot, almost brutal desperation. He groaned deep in his throat as his mouth opened. His tongue entered her: hot, moist, urgent.

He lifted his head. "Sacha, I didn't want—" His lips met her own again. "Don't let me do this— It's not what—" His tongue traced the pouty curve of her lower lip. His hands suddenly slid around her, cupping the pert cheeks of her bottom. He squeezed slowly, rhythmically, his tongue licking teasingly at her lower lip. "I love the feel of you," he whispered. "So firm." He suddenly lifted her with both hands. "Put your legs around me."

She obeyed, clutching his shoulders desperately as he pressed her to him. She gave a low cry as she pushed mindlessly against him. "This is even—" She forgot what she had been about to say as he shifted, rubbing against the heart of her womanhood. Fire. Heat. Male. "Brody, I think . . ."

"Stop thinking," he muttered, his cheek burning against her own. "Heaven knows, I have. Just let me come into you. I'm hurting so."

"Yes." She instinctively nestled closer and felt another shudder rack him. "I told you it was all right." She tenderly smoothed the hair at his nape. "I want to give to you."

He froze. She could feel the stiffening of his muscles hardening against her. "Brody?"

He was suddenly shifting her, carrying her toward the bed. A surge of relief went through her.

He dropped her on the bed and jerked the satin sheet up over her.

His light eyes were blazing down into her own.

"I don't want you *giving* me anything, dammit. How can I make you understand? Just once I wanted to give something to someone else without asking what was in it for me."

"You did give me something," she whispered. "My life."

"Dammit, Sacha, listen to me. I'm not going to let you—" He broke off as he saw the glittering brightness of her eyes. "Hell!" He turned on his heel and strode toward the door. "You stay here. I'll take the guest room tonight."

She struggled to a sitting position, her hands trembling as they clutched the silk sheet. Cold. The silk was so icy against her after Brody's fiery warmth. "You don't understand," she said huskily.

"You're right. I don't understand a damn thing about you and I'm so damn horny, it's a wonder I can even think at all." He opened the door. "We'll talk about this tomorrow morning." The door slammed behind him.

Sacha stared at the door for a long time. Two tears brimmed in her eyes and then ran slowly down her cheeks. "You just don't understand, Brody."

"Mr. Devlin." The knock on the door was as hesitant as Levine's voice. "I'm sorry to wake you, but we may have a slight problem."

Brody came wide-awake and raised himself on one elbow. Sacha? What else could it be? His life had been one problem after another since Sacha had come on the scene. "Come in, Levine. What the hell is wrong now?"

Barry Levine stuck his head in the door. "We just wondered if you knew Miss Lorion has left the grounds. She said she needed something from the grocery store and one of my men gave her a lift to the supermarket. But I thought maybe I should check with you since Mr. Radison said she was to stay here under tight security."

"Grocery store?" Brody repeated blankly. "I practically bought out the supermarket last night. She couldn't have needed—" He threw off the sheet and began to dress hurriedly. "How long ago did she leave?"

"About ten minutes." Levine shifted uneasily. "Carp is a good man, Mr. Devlin. He'll keep her safe."

If Sacha gave the man the chance to protect her. Brody had a sudden memory of Sacha's pale, strained face last night before he had left her. Panic exploded within him. "Get Carp on the car radio and tell him not to leave her alone for a minute. Not for a second."

"He wouldn't do that anyway," Levine protested. "I told you he was a good—"

"*Tell him,*" Brody said between set teeth as he headed for the bathroom. "And tell Harris I want the car out front in three minutes."

Levine was back in less than two minutes, his expression alarmed. "Mr. Devlin, I don't know how to tell you this. Miss Lorion—"

"Is missing," Brody snapped grimly.

"But it wasn't our fault this time. Carp thinks she ran out the back door of the supermarket when she sent him to get a basket. How can we be expected to protect someone who deliberately tries to give us the slip?" Levine ruffled his sandy hair distractedly. "Lord, Mr. Randal is going to have our heads in a handbasket."

"If Randal doesn't, I will." Brody brushed past him as he headed for the front door. "You shouldn't have let her leave here." He knew he wasn't being fair, but at the moment he didn't give a damn. It didn't matter that Levine and his men couldn't know Sacha would run away. She was *gone*, and the guilt and fear made him want to strike out at everyone. "Radio Carp and tell him he's to search the entire area. You and the rest of your men follow me."

"You think you know where she's going?"

"I hope I do." If he was right, Sacha would run to the only familiar person she knew in this country: Louis Benoit. "The Majestic Hotel."

Seven

"Where is she, Benoit?" Brody demanded as soon
as the Frenchman stepped from the elevator into
the lobby. "Dammit, you know she isn't safe here."

Louis nodded. "It would not have been my choice
for her to return here. If you can't convince her to
go back with you, we will have to leave immediately."

Brody felt a surge of relief so strong, it almost
made him dizzy. "Then she *is* here!"

"She arrived about twenty minutes ago." Louis
shook his head. "You handled the situation very
clumsily, Devlin. You should have expected her to
leave when you gave her nothing to hold on to."

Brody stiffened. "She told you what happened
last night?"

Louis shrugged. "Of course, why not?" He

glanced at Levine standing next to Brody. "Can we be alone? We need to talk."

"The only thing I need is for you to tell me where to find Sacha," Brody said, trying to leash the sudden fury he was experiencing. She had actually told Benoit she had tried to seduce another man, and all he did was shrug it off as casually as if it were a commonplace occurrence. No jealousy, no indignation, not even a raised eyebrow. "That blasted desk clerk wouldn't give us your room number."

"We have an agreement," Louis said cynically. "You should have offered him a bribe, instead of threatening him. It works much better with some people. Send your man away. You'll get nothing from me with either threats or bribes until we talk." He met Brody's gaze steadily. "Sacha doesn't know you're here. When I got your call from the desk, I decided it would be better to come down and discuss this before you barged in and blew everything again."

"I once asked Sacha if you were her pimp," Brody said, being deliberately insulting. "She said you weren't, but you're acting remarkably like one at the moment."

A swift flare of anger lit Louis's dark eyes. "I'm no pimp." He was obviously trying to control his temper. "But I know Sacha and I care what happens to her. I think you do, too, or we wouldn't be having this conversation." His smile was a tigerish baring of teeth. "Instead, I would be thinking of ways to mutilate your famous face."

Levine took a protective step closer to Brody. "I could talk to the manager, Mr. Devlin. Enough pressure and—"

"No," Brody cut him short, his gaze never leaving Louis's face. "Go back to the car, Barry."

Levine frowned. "I don't think—"

Brody made an impatient gesture. "If I need you, I'll send for you."

Levine hesitated, then turned on his heel and strode through the lobby toward the front entrance.

"Well?" Brody asked.

Louis gestured to a small room opening off the lobby. "No one should be in the bar this early in the day, not even the bartender. Pity. I'd let you buy me a drink. I could use one." He moved gracefully into the dimness of the deserted bar and sat down at a white plastic table to the right of the door. "I'm not accustomed to interfering in Sacha's life. She's the only friend I have, and I don't take risks with that friendship."

Brody sat down opposite him. "Talk."

"Americans are so direct." Louis leaned back in his chair and gazed at Brody with a faint smile. "You're angry with me. Why is that? It is you who made Sacha run away. You should have taken what she offered. It was stupid of you to think she would let you help her without giving something in return."

"You're saying I should have made Sacha my mistress?" Brody's voice was threaded with fury. "What the hell kind of man are you?"

"One who wants to keep Sacha alive," Louis

said quietly. "I thought we were agreed about that. You took a bullet for her two nights ago."

"That doesn't mean I want her paying me by jumping into the sack with me."

"You told her that you desired her and you're a very rich man. It was the only coin she could be sure you actually wanted."

"I didn't tell her that to make her—" Brody broke off in helpless exasperation. "Dear Lord, what a mess."

"Yes, and one that must be cleaned up if Sacha is to remain safe. It's not entirely your fault. Sacha should have told you more about herself, and you would have understood what a mistake it would be for you to refuse her." Benoit smiled sadly. "I think perhaps she is a little afraid to tell you about her past. She says she is not, but it's natural that she would be uncertain. You must make her tell you." He paused. "I cannot do it for her. I don't have the right, but there's one thing I can tell you. Sacha and I are not lovers."

Brody became still. "I find that hard to believe. You sleep in the same bed."

Louis's expression was suddenly shuttered. "It was convenient at times." He shrugged. "Our relationship is rather complicated. She will tell you."

"Perhaps," Brody said. "But I think I'd rather hear it from you."

"Too bad." Louis pushed back his chair and stood up. "I have told you enough. It is Sacha we must be concerned about now. You can not imagine what she has gone through in her life. It must be ended." His voice grew more harsh. "So, dammit, forget your idiotic reservations and keep Sacha with you where she'll be safe and we have a chance of capturing Gino. If she wants to go to bed with you, let her." He started to turn toward the door and then stopped. He reached into his pocket, pulled out a large brass key, and tossed it on the table. "Sacha is in Room Two-oh-three. I'll give you thirty minutes. I hope you're both gone when I get back. Tell her I said it was time she told you everything."

Brody's hand closed on the key. "What if she refuses? I'm not going to leave her here even if I have to have Levine's men tie her hand and foot and cart her out of the hotel."

Louis frowned. "No, she must come to you willingly. Sacha has had much practice in hiding. If she leaves you again, you will not find her."

Brody felt a chill touch him to the very bone. "She's not going to run away again. I'll find a way of keeping her with me."

"Not unless you begin to understand what causes Sacha to be what she is." Louis frowned thoughtfully. "There has to be a trigger to make her tell you." Something flickered in his eyes as the answer came to him. "Have you ever noticed that whenever Sacha is frightened or nervous, she rubs behind her left ear?"

Brody nodded slowly, puzzled.

"Make her show you what's behind her ear." Louis turned and walked out of the bar.

• • •

Sacha was sitting on the bed when Brody swung open the door of the hotel room. She straightened with shock, her eyes wide in her pale face. "Brody, what are you doing here?"

"Where did you expect me to be?" He stepped into the room and shut the door. "Every time I turn around, you're gone. Did you think I'd just let you run away? Your friend Louis tells me I'm an idiot, but I'll—"

"Louis gave you his key," Sacha interrupted. "He should not have done that. You don't understand."

"That's what you told me last night." Brody pocketed the key and walked toward her. "And you were right. I don't understand a damn thing, but it's not because I don't want to. I've been wandering around in the dark from the moment I first met you, and I'm tired of being understanding and not asking questions. I want to know what the hell is going on."

"I know I haven't been fair, Brody, but I didn't think . . ." She rubbed behind her ear. "I don't know— What are you doing?"

Brody's hands were carefully lifting the silken strands of her hair and pulling it back from her left ear. "Obeying instructions. Benoit told me to look behind your—" He inhaled sharply. "My God!" Four small white scars formed a crescent on the tender flesh just behind her ear. Each was perfectly round and of an identical size. "These are from burns!"

Sacha hurriedly stepped back and pushed his

hands away. "Louis had no right to tell you to do this."

"He refused to tell me anything else." His gaze was fixed on her ear, now half veiled by the curving bell of her page boy. "He said you'd tell me the rest." He swallowed hard. He felt sick. "What caused those burns, Sacha?"

She looked away from him. "What does it matter? They're very old burns. It happened a long time ago."

"It matters. What, Sacha?"

Her gaze returned to him and she smiled shakily. "You're going to be difficult again, aren't you?"

"Oh, yes," he said huskily. "Damn difficult. How did you get those scars?"

She hesitated and then abruptly gave in. "Gino smokes a cigar."

Shock and rage exploded within him. "That bastard *burned* you with a lighted cigar?"

She nodded. "I disobeyed him, and he decided he had to set an example." She shivered. "Gino is a great one for examples. Every day that I came back without money, he tied me in a chair and had one of the other children hold my hair." She moistened her lips with her tongue. "He did it very slowly and only one burn for each offense. Then he would untie me and give me a hug and a piece of candy. I can remember him laughing and telling me that all bad children must be punished, but he loved me anyway."

"Children? How old were you?"

"Seven."

She heard his soft curse and her gaze went to

his face. His expression held such menace, it shocked her. "It only happened that first week I came to Paris. I gave in after the fourth day and he never burned me again."

"How magnanimous of him." Brody's voice held tones of silken savagery that were chilling, Sacha thought. "He only tortured you four times. And just what did you do to keep in his good graces?"

"I picked pockets," she said simply. "We all did."

"We?"

"There were usually anywhere from ten to fifteen of us at the trailer encampment at one time." Her face clouded. "When one of us reached the age of thirteen, Gino couldn't use him anymore as a pickpocket, so he sold him into prostitution." She shuddered. "I know I couldn't let that happen to me. I saw what they became. No freedom. No hope."

"Who the hell is this Gino? How could he get away with this? It sounds like something out of *Oliver Twist.*"

"It was a little like that, I suppose. Sometimes it wasn't a bad life. Children usually find a way of adjusting, and we were free to roam the streets and play as long as we brought home our quota of francs every day. I met Louis the first week I was there. He was a year older than I was and had been in Paris about six months. He tried to persuade Gino not to burn me." She made a face. "He didn't succeed, of course, and ended up with a split lip himself. The second night Gino made him hold back my hair when he burned me. I remember the tears were running down Louis's cheeks. . . ."

Brody felt tears sting his own eyes. "How could it happen?" he asked again. "Where was your grandfather?"

"He was the one who sold me to Gino," she said simply. "I told you he hated *gajos.* When my mother died and he found the letter, he went into a rage. He never wanted to see me again and he thought he might as well profit by it. There are gypsy 'bosses' like Gino in practically every major city in Europe who use bands of children to rob the tourists. The money we brought in wasn't as little as you might think. I know Gino had investments in several housing developments in Madrid and Marseilles." She shrugged. "High profits and low upkeep. He might have gone on for a long time if I hadn't found enough evidence to get the gendarmes to prosecute. I was almost twelve by that time and Louis was thirteen." Her voice was only a level above a whisper. "I was so frightened the night at the hospital when the X-ray technician came in and told the police sergeant that Louis was thirteen. I knew Gino would—"

"X rays? I don't understand," Brody said gently. "You're getting ahead of yourself, Sacha."

"I'm sorry. I'll try to be more clear." She paused, attempting to marshal her thoughts. "You see, according to French law, we were safe from prosecution as long as we were under thirteen. The police usually rounded us up and took us to the station at least once a month, but they always let us go. Occasionally they'd send us to the hospital to have our hands X-rayed." She laughed shakily. "One of the miracles of modern medicine. Gino always made us lie to the police about our age but they could tell how old we were from the X rays. Anyway, the police were told that Louis was thirteen or older, and I knew Jacques would tell Gino. Jacques was Gino's informant among us. He was given extra food, toys, and blankets in exchange for making sure Gino knew everything that was going on. I was praying the police sergeant would arrest Louis, but he let him off with a warning." Her voice lowered to a level above a whisper. "And Gino was waiting outside the hospital in a van to pick us up. Louis disappeared the next night, like all the others when they reached thirteen." She closed her eyes. "I was terrified, but I knew I had to do something. I couldn't let them hurt Louis. I stole Gino's account books and went to the police."

"They caught him?" There was fierce satisfaction in Brody's voice. "God, I hope they sent him straight to prison."

Sacha shook her head. "He had the money to hire a good lawyer. Even though I was a material witness, he got only ten years. They couldn't connect him with the prostitution. It was over a year before the police found Louis in a bordello in Venice." Her lids opened to reveal eyes glittering with tears. "Poor Louis. He doesn't talk about that time, but it . . . changed him. He won't let anyone close to him now."

"What happened after the trial?"

"The police found us a place in a charity home and sent us to school. We got on with our lives and trained for careers. Louis is quite wonderful at mathematics. He'll be a financial wizard one day."

"And you?"

"I was studying dress designing and doing a little photographic modeling on the side. I'm a pretty good designer, by the way."

Brody had to swallow to ease the tightness of his throat. "I'm sure you are. When did Gino get out of prison?"

"A little over two months ago. We weren't expecting it. We should have had another year before we had to worry about him." Her lips twisted wearily. "I guess I shouldn't have been surprised. Gino always was clever. The police warned us that he was looking for us and gave Louis and me tickets and documents to get us to America." She drew a deep breath and smiled with an effort. "There, now you know it all."

He shook his head. "No, not all." He smoothed back her hair and with infinite tenderness rubbed the scarred flesh behind her left ear. "There's still one thing I don't know. Why should anyone who has suffered as much as you have think she has to pay someone to keep her safe? Can't you see that you deserve it? You've paid your dues. Let someone take care of you for a change."

"You?" she whispered. "I can't, Brody. Don't you see? For five years I *stole* from people. I hated it, but I did it. I even made sure I was good

enough so that I could steal more than my share.
That way I could give it to any one of the other
children who didn't manage to meet the quota.
Do you know how doing that made me feel? I
can't steal anything ever again, and taking without giving is stealing."

"Sacha . . ." Brody trailed off helplessly. She
meant it. No matter what arguments he used he
would never be able to sway her from her deep
conviction. "You're making this impossible for me."

"I never meant to do so. I only wanted to help,
Brody."

"I know." Tenderness moved through him in an
aching tide. "I know you well enough to realize
that now, Sacha. You won't change your mind?"

She shook her head without speaking.

"Then it looks like I'm going to have to change
mine, doesn't it?" He kissed her lightly on the tip
of her nose. "So much for nobility. You win,
Sacha."

"What?"

"You're coming home with me."

"No, I told you—"

He placed two fingers on her lips to stop her.
"You want to give? Okay. I'm taking." His gaze
flicked to the double bed and then back to her. "I
hope you won't insist on our consummating our
deal here. I had another place in mind."

She was staring at him, her eyes wide, scarcely
breathing. "You mean it?"

"Oh, yes, I mean it." Something heated flared in
the depths of his eyes. "I'm going to take you to

bed and let you give me anything you choose." His lips curved in a reckless smile. "And maybe a few things I choose. I'm tired of fighting against my own nature." He picked up her purse from the bed and handed it to her. "Shall we go?"

"It's not a trick?" she whispered.

"You want proof?" He reached out and began to unbutton her white shirt. He unfastened the front catch of her bra and pushed it slowly aside to reveal her naked breasts. "Don't wear a bra again. You don't need one, and it will only get in the way"—he lowered his head with leisurely deliberateness—"when I want to do this." His mouth opened and then closed over one taut nipple.

She cried out, arching forward as she felt his warm tongue teasing the hard tip. His hand cupped her other breast, his thumb and forefinger pulling rhythmically as he stroked her with his tongue. "Brody . . ."

But he wasn't listening. His lips were suckling strongly now, biting gently and then soothing the teasing abrasion with his tongue. When he finally raised his head her nipples were pointed, distended, and as blazing as the color mantling her cheeks.

He stared at the swollen beauty of her breasts for a long time before his gaze lifted to her face. "Do you believe me now?"

She couldn't speak, but managed to nod wordlessly.

"Good. Then we'd better get out of here, or I may change my mind. That lumpy bed is beginning to look very inviting." He fastened her bra and quickly buttoned her blouse. "Did you have a jacket?"

She gestured vaguely. "On the chair."

He crossed the room and returned with the blue-jean jacket. "I think you'd better put this on." His gaze lingered on the tips of her breasts pressing hard against the fabric of her bra and straining against the cotton of the white shirt. "Not that I don't enjoy seeing you like this." He skimmed his fingertips teasingly over her breasts and chuckled as he saw the sudden thrusting response. "But I'd prefer no one else noticed." He helped her on with the jacket. "Once we're in the car, it won't matter. We'll roll up the glass, and Harris is far too discreet ever to look in the rearview mirror."

"In the limousine? You're going to . . . ?"

His lids half veiled his eyes, and he smiled with a blatant sensuality that caused her heart to skip a beat and then begin to pound erratically. "Perhaps someday. It might be very erotic. Today we'll just play a little to increase the anticipation while we're driving to our little love nest."

"Malibu?"

He shook his head as he turned her toward the door. "Not Malibu. I don't think I could wait that long. I know a place that's much closer to the hotel."

"The theater?" Sacha asked blankly.

The limousine rolled to a stop in the alley at the

backstage door. Harris hopped out of the driver's seat and opened the passenger door.

"I thought it fitting," Brody said quietly. "You didn't like the house in Malibu, and you may learn a few things about me here." He got out and held out his hand to help her from the car before turning to Harris. "When Levine and his men show up, tell them to wait here for us. We may be quite a while."

"Sure." Harris nodded. "You bet, Mr. Devlin."

"It's not fair to keep him waiting," Sacha whispered as Brody's hand on her elbow propelled her toward the stage entrance. "Perhaps we should—"

"No, Sacha, we are *not* inviting him to come in with us. Dinner is one thing, but I'm not planning a cozy social get-together this time." He pulled open the door and stepped into the shadowy hallway. "They can all wait outside."

"No one is allowed here now without authorization." A short, wiry man with curly red hair was hurrying toward them. "You can't—" He broke off, an apologetic grin creasing his thin cheeks. "Hello, Mr. Devlin. It's so damn dark in here, I didn't recognize you. The manager is stingy as hell about the electric bills between engagements. Now, what can I do for you? I didn't expect to see you here again after the closing last night."

"Hello, Billy." Brody smiled with beguiling warmth at the man. "Sacha, this is Billy Bodeen. Sacha Lorion. Miss Lorion is very interested in set design, Billy. I thought I'd let her study the *Camelot* sets, if they're still here."

Billy nodded. "The costumes and sets aren't due to be packed and shipped back to New York until Monday. They're all back in the storage room."

"Good. Then I'll take Miss Lorion there to take a look. You just go on with whatever you were doing. We might be some time. Miss Lorion may become very involved." Brody waved casually before pushing Sacha ahead of him down the hall. "In fact, I'm quite sure she will. Thanks, Billy."

"No problem," Bodeen said. "Just remember to turn off the lights or I'll be on the carpet with management."

"I'll remember," Brody said over his shoulder. His steps quickened as he strode down the hall with Sacha in tow.

"Set design?" Sacha murmured.

He shrugged. "Set design, dress design. It's only a small prevarication." They had reached a mahogany door twice as wide as an ordinary entrance at the end of the corridor. He paused with his hand on the knob to smile down at her with heart-stopping charm. "I did try to stick to the truth for the most part. I have every intention of making sure we don't leave here for a long, long time." He opened the door and stepped aside to let her precede him. "After you, love."

She cast him an uncertain glance before stepping before him into the large, cluttered room. The ceiling arched a good fifty feet above the dimness of the storage room and was illuminated by only two narrow windows high on the north wall. The early-afternoon sunlight streamed through the windows like two golden beacons, dancing motes of dust bringing a deceptive aura of life to the bold bands of illumination.

Sacha gazed around her with fascination as she took a tentative step forward. Secrets. Secrets revealed. Secrets kept. Painted background sets could be discerned in the dimness. Arthur's tree, from where he had first spied upon Guenevere. The elaborate glitter of the two thrones might well be gold if one failed to look too closely. The battlefield tent from the last scene. The Sword Excalibur lying carelessly across the cushions of a stool.

"Not so glamorous close up, is it?" Brody followed her into the room and shot the bolt on the door. "It's all make-believe, Sacha."

There was a curiously somber note in his voice that made her turn and look at him. "Why did you bring me here, Brody?"

"I thought it might amuse you." He smiled crookedly. "And I remembered it had the required equipment for what you had in mind." He crossed the room, a stream of sunlight through a high window tangling in his hair and setting it aflame. Then he was once again embraced by shadows. "Come here, Sacha."

Her eyes narrowed, trying to see him as she followed his voice from sunlight to shadow. "I'm coming. Where are you? I can't—" She broke off as she caught sight of him.

He was standing by a canopy bed hung with white velvet drapes and a coverlet of matching velvet. "You remember Lancelot's tryst in Guenevere's bedchamber, don't you? Unfortunately poor Lancelot never got to use this bed before the guards arrived." He patted the velvet counterpane. "It's just as well; the mattress is hard as a rock. It didn't matter because it was only for show anyway."

"Are you trying to tell me something?" She drew a quivering breath. "I'm afraid I'm too nervous at the moment to decipher obscure messages. You'll have to speak more plainly if you want me to understand."

"It's all for show. It's make-believe." He paused. "And so am I, Sacha. I'm not your brother, and I'm not King Arthur. I'm only an actor who probably has as little real substance as the sword lying over there on that stool. Maybe these props are more real than I am, because lately the only times I've felt alive were when I was playing a part." He shrugged wearily. "I guess it's the only place I feel I have real worth."

"Why are you telling me this?" Sacha asked softly.

A muscle jerked in his cheek. "Because you deserve better than me. Listen, nobody cared about me when I was a kid either. My life was a little like yours as far as that goes. My mother and father were both too interested in their careers to bother about a child. But I wasn't like you. Instead of reaching out to the people around me, I withdrew into myself. Then I discovered acting and I withdrew into that. You think you know me, but you don't. I'm not sure there's anything to know.

Sometimes I think I'm a ghost, a chimera composed of all the parts I've ever played. But you're real, Sacha, and I don't want to hurt you, dammit. Please. Change your mind." His hands clenched slowly at his sides. "Because I don't think I'll let you go if we use this bed. I'll keep taking until you get tired and send me away."

She stood gazing at him, her expression one of almost maternal tenderness. How little he knew himself, she thought. He said he wasn't like Arthur, yet he was exhibiting a remarkably similar taste for self-sacrifice. She felt a sudden golden explosion of feeling that thrilled even as it frightened her. Oh, dear, not this too. Why hadn't she realized that she loved him not as a brother but as the one man to complete her? She *mustn't* love him like this.

His stance was charged with tension. "Well?"

She should run away. It would be the intelligent thing to do. They were worlds apart. He might never come to love her as she did him. Yet even as she gave herself this wise advice she knew she wouldn't take it. A short time with Brody would be better than nothing, and when had she ever relied on logic instead of instinct? She took a step forward. "I don't get bored very easily. I think that's the sign of a boring person." She tried to smile. "And I think chimeras must be quite interesting once you get to know them." She plopped down on the bed and bounced up and down to test the mattress. "And this bed isn't really that hard." She didn't look at him as she took off her jacket, slipped off her shoes, and began to unbutton her blouse. "And I think it's rather romantic to be here on—"

"No romance, Sacha," he cut in harshly. "Sex. Don't fool yourself it's going to be anything else."

Her gaze lifted to his. "No illusions at all?"

He started to shake his head, his expression strangely stern. Then, as he detected wistfulness in her, he stopped and said quickly, "Dammit, don't look like that." He sat down beside her and cupped her face in his palms. "Perhaps a few illusions wouldn't hurt," he said softly. "As long as we realize what we're doing. What would you like to pretend, Sacha? What role would you like me to play?"

The role of a man who would love her forever, she wanted to tell him. "I don't care," she said in a tone that was almost inaudible. "You're a spellbinder in whatever role you play. You choose."

He bent slowly until his lips were only a breath away from her own. When he spoke, his lips brushed hers with a gossamer kiss punctuating every word. "Then I choose not to play at all. The spellbinder is on vacation." His warm tongue lightly outlined her lower lip. She inhaled sharply and a throbbing began wherever his tongue touched her. Her lips felt suddenly full, swollen, exquisitely sensitive. "This is only a man." He lifted his head, and the look in his eyes was like the room around them. Sunlight and shadow, ghost and substance, an emptiness that overflowed and became . . . loneliness. "Make me real. I want to be real for you, Sacha."

"You are real," she said shakily. "If you became any more real, I think I might melt into a puddle on this fine velvet spread."

His eyes suddenly twinkled. "I don't think I have to worry about that. I've noticed you always have both feet on the ground." He pushed her back on the bed. "A state I'm about to correct. That position might prove to be a bit inconvenient for what we have in mind." He removed her shirt and bra, then looked down at her. "Lord, you're pretty, love."

She wrinkled her nose at him. "I'm no Dolly Parton. You always asked for women with large breasts when you called Marceline's."

He lowered his lips to tug at one pert nipple. "I've changed my mind. Small breasts can be quite erotic when you add a certain dimension." His hand cupped and squeezed rhythmically. "Sort of a do-it-yourself project." Her breasts were swelling, firming, beneath his hands and mouth. She couldn't breathe; she was almost panting for air as his teeth nipped at the engorged peak.

He lifted his head, his eyes glazed and hot as he looked at his work. "And it definitely gives a man a certain feeling of accomplishment." His hand moved down to unfasten her jeans. The zipper slid sibilantly, the sound sending a shiver through her. His gaze left her breasts and traveled up to study her face. "Are you excited?"

She gazed at him helplessly. "Yes."

"How excited?" he asked. "Tell me."

She could scarcely speak, her throat was so tight. "I think you know."

He lifted her hips to strip off her jeans and the bikini panties beneath them before tossing the garments carelessly aside. "But it's fun to hear the words. Haven't you found that out?"

"No, I've never—" She stopped. "What do you want me to say?"

"Anything you like." His palm teasingly rubbed the tight curls surrounding her womanhood. "This feels so good. I've just thought of another item of clothing I want you to stop wearing."

"Pretty soon you won't have me wearing anything."

"Probably." His fingers wandered down to stroke, toy, and rotate. The muscles of her stomach clenched, and she made a sound that was a half gasp, half moan. "But think how convenient it would be. You'd like it too. I'd make sure you liked it." Two fingers plunged into the heart of her, and her body arched helplessly up toward him in a motion as old as desire. "Just think about it. We'd be walking along the beach, and all I'd have to do would be to pull you behind a dune and lift your skirt." The rhythm of his fingers quickened. "And do this. It would be so easy."

"It doesn't feel easy," she gasped through clenched teeth. Shivers of fire were quivering through her. . . . She felt as if she were exploding, burning. She couldn't think. Brody's deep, mesmerizing voice was painting pictures that she felt as well as envisioned. Hot sun stroking her body, white dunes hiding them from the world. And the rhythm—"It feels . . . hard."

He stopped. "But good?"

Her hips moved yearningly. "Yes."

"Roll over."

"What?" she asked vaguely.

His hands left her and he stood up. "Roll over, love," he said softly. "You'll like this, too, I promise you." He pulled his black sweatshirt over his head and threw it aside. He smiled coaxingly. "For me?"

Who could refuse him when he smiled so sweetly? She rolled over on her stomach and felt suddenly very vulnerable now that she couldn't see him. She heard the sound of his undressing and the deep harshness of his labored breathing. She could smell his musky maleness, but she couldn't *see* him. "Brody?"

"I'm here." He was beside her on the bed again, his lips brushing the exact center of her lower spine. An excited shudder quivered through her. His palms began kneading the pert swelling of her buttocks. "You have a wonderful derriere. That first night I met you, I was thinking I'd like to see you like this." His teeth nipped sharply at one rounded cheek. No pain, just a flicker of liquid heat between her thighs. "Do you like this?"

"I'm not sure. I feel . . . helpless."

"Do you? In a moment I'm the one who's going to be helpless. Part your legs, love. Let me come into you." He was moving her, coming between her thighs, lifting her, invading her.

She cried out in surprise, then bit her lower lip in annoyance.

Brody stopped. "Did I hurt you?"

"No." It was true. Heat. Fullness. Not pain.

"You're so tight," he muttered. "I didn't expect . . . Tell me if I hurt you."

His hands slid around to cup her breasts in the palms, his thumb and fingers plucking at her nipples, his breath feathering her ear as he braced himself on his knees. "We'll lie like this in the dunes and the sand will be warm and rough against you." His tongue toyed with the lobe of her ear. "And I'll be warm and rough inside you." He plunged deep!

This time she kept from crying out, but it was impossible to mask the betrayal of her body.

He froze. "Sacha, my God. . . ."

She was glad her face was hidden from his. "It doesn't hurt." Her voice was muffled in the pillow. "I like it." She suddenly bucked upward, clenching around him. "Go on."

"Sacha." Her name was a low groan. "Don't . . ."

She clenched again. "Go on!"

He muttered something beneath his breath. "Dammit, Sacha."

She felt his shudder within her body. "It doesn't matter."

"The hell it doesn't," he said thickly. "But not enough to stop me. Not now." He drove forward and began a wild, tempestuous rhythm that rocked her to the foundations of her being. Her hands clenched into fists. She tried to help him, but his pace was too furious, too wild. Fullness. Beauty. Brody. Always Brody. Passion. Fire. Spellbinder.

His breathing harshened above her until it was nearly a sob. "Sacha, I can't wait any longer."

Neither could she. The spiraling tension snapped, exploding into a million sunlit shards. She heard Brody's low guttural cry above her. He collapsed against her, his chest lifting and falling against her back, his words spaced by gasps that made his voice almost inaudible. "Sacha, I never felt anything like that before. You nearly tore me apart."

She laughed huskily. "I think you've stolen my line. Isn't that what I'm supposed to say?"

Brody stiffened against her. "That's right, it is." He moved off her quickly. "Turn over, dammit. We have some talking to do."

Eight

Sacha sighed contentedly and then lazily turned over to look at him. How beautiful he was, she thought tenderly. His rumpled chestnut hair gave him an air of boyishness that was in strange contrast to the mature masculinity of his tough, muscular body. The bronze of his skin appeared much darker in the hazy half-light illuminating the room, and his eyes shone a more brilliant shade of blue.

"I liked that very much," she said softly. "But next time could we do it in a way that makes it possible for me to watch your face? I think I would enjoy that even more."

He muttered a low curse and jumped up from the bed. "What the hell would you say if I said no?" He strode over to the huge wardrobe trunk against the far wall and threw it open with barely contained violence. He jerked out a velvet surcoat in a shade of rich chocolate-brown and pulled it on. "What if I said I'd rather have you on your head or maybe—" He stopped and leaned his forehead against the side of the trunk. "Dammit, Sacha, why didn't you tell me?"

"It wasn't important, and I knew you would feel guilty about making love to a virgin." She smiled. "You're far more noble than you think you are. And it wasn't as though I were saving myself or anything. I'm merely very selective."

"And so you 'selected' a man who's been notorious for his sexual escapades since he was a teenager. Not very smart, Sacha. There's no telling what I could have asked you to do."

"I'm sure you wouldn't have done anything that would hurt me or that I wouldn't have enjoyed." She frowned. "I didn't mean to complain before. You have a wonderful face, and I would have liked to watch your expressions, but if you really prefer to—"

"Sacha, for heaven's sake, be *still*." His voice was muffled. "Now isn't the time for you to . . ." He reached into the wardrobe and riffled through the costumes. "I've never even had a virgin. I didn't think there were any over fifteen these days. I can't think."

"It's very foolish of you to be so upset. I didn't know you could be this old-fashioned."

He found the garment he was looking for and jerked it from the hanger. "I'm not old-fashioned; I'm merely a little disconcerted." There was a thread of indignation in his voice as he turned and came back toward her. "I'm not accustomed to situations of this type." He stopped halfway to the bed as a thought occurred to him. "This should make us quits. You don't owe me anything now. Even trade."

Her laughter rang out, echoing in the enormous room. "Oh, no, Brody. Not even at all. I told you my inexperience was not important. Our arrangement stands."

A flicker of emotion touched his face, which was a mixture of frustration, sadness, and relief. "Sacha . . ." He came toward her. "Sit up and let me put this on you."

She knelt on the bed and gazed at the loose sapphire velvet robe in his hand. "That's Guenevere's robe in the bedroom scene. She looked quite beautiful in it." She slipped her arms into the wide sleeves, her fingertips caressing the white ermine trim that bordered the robe. "Blondes always look lovely in blue."

"Do they?" He fastened the ermine-covered button at her throat and arranged the shining bell of her hair to free it of the jeweled collar. "I think it looks better on you." He stood gazing at her and felt a familiar tightening of his throat. Her eyes—clear, honest, and warm with humor and joy—gazed back at him. His hands moved from her hair to cup her face gently. "Sacha, Sacha, what am I supposed to do with you? "

Her face was suddenly alight with mischief. "You should know better than I, but I think you've done it. We have only to repeat. First, though, I believe it would be nice if you held me. I understand that is pleasant also."

He sat down on the bed and pulled her into his arms. "Like this?" His voice was husky. He rocked her gently back and forth, his lips brushing her temple. "Anything else, milady? Perhaps I should break into a few verses of "How to Handle a Woman." Though I wouldn't recommend it. A voice like mine needs all the help it can get from the orchestra."

"You do very well." Her palm stroked the softness of his dark brown velvet surcoat. She was content enough to purr as her cheek nestled dreamily against his shoulder. "Though I never really understood why you took the part. It's so much lighter than the roles you usually choose."

"I wasn't going to do it." His hand came up beneath her hair to rub the tendons of her nape. "I was prepared to turn it down right up to the very last page of the script. Then I came to Arthur's speech to the boy Tom. Do you remember? He talks about mankind as less than a drop of water in the sunlit sea."

"I remember."

"And then he says, 'Some of the drops do sparkle.' He was a man with a broken dream, but he could still see hope shining in the darkness. I liked that. I think this weary old world needs all the hope we can bring to it."

"Yet you claim you're a hardened cynic," she whispered. "I don't believe a cynic would take a role just because it was about hope."

"Maybe not." His tone was self-mocking. "Maybe I really took it because I wanted to show the world how versatile I was. Vanity, pure and simple."

"No," she protested. "It wasn't for that reason. Why do you—"

"You don't think I'm versatile?" He bore her back on the bed. "I'm always willing to demonstrate." His fingers were at her throat, unfastening the ermine closing he had so recently buttoned. His eyes darkened and his mockery vanished as he parted the robe and looked down at her. "If milady permits?"

She could feel the heated tension start to spiral within her. The world was beginning to narrow down to checkered sunlight and Brody's intent eyes gazing down at her. "Milady applauds," she said, and reached up to touch his cheek with a fingertip. "Could I see your face this time?"

He turned his head to catch her finger between his lips. "I'm not sure I want you to. You see entirely too much, and I don't know if I care to be vulnerable to anyone."

"I'm vulnerable but I'm not afraid."

He nibbled at her fingers, not looking at her. Then his gaze swung back to her, and she experienced a little shock at what she saw there. It couldn't be. . . . Then whatever emotion had been revealed was first veiled and then gone and she realized she must have been mistaken. "But you're braver than I, Sacha." He parted her legs and moved between them. "I thought you realized that by now." The expression on his face was half sad, half tender, as he looked down at her. "But I'll try to have a little of your courage." His lips lowered until their lips were only a breath away. "Because I want to watch your face, too, love."

The drive back to Malibu was almost silent, and Brody was curiously remote and abstracted.

Sacha gazed at him in puzzlement. "Is something wrong?"

"What?" Brody's gaze left the view passing by the window. "Oh, no. Everything's fine. I was just thinking." He reached over to take her hand and raise it to his lips. "I had a few decisions to make."

"The movie or the Broadway play? Which did you decide on?"

He lowered his gaze to her hand. "I definitely decided on the play."

"When do the rehearsals start?"

"I'm not sure," he said vaguely. "I'll have to see about making arrangements." His gaze returned to the scene outside the window. "Soon." He didn't speak again until Harris drew up before the white stone–and–glass modernistic house and Brody had helped her from the car. "You go on inside." He glanced back over his shoulder at the black Ford sedan coming up the winding cliff road. "I want to have a word with Levine. Why don't you make us a light lunch?"

"You're hungry?"

"Starved," he said absently, his gaze never leaving Levine's car. "Run along now."

"All right." She started up the steps. "A salad and sandwiches?"

"Anything."

The Ford had pulled up in front of the garage, and Brody walked toward it.

Sacha paused uncertainly, her hand on the knob of the door. Brody had been behaving most peculiarly since they had left the theater, and now he was obviously trying to get rid of her. Barry Levine had gotten out of the car, and Brody was standing next to him, speaking to him in low, rapid sentences that were inaudible to Sacha from where she was standing.

She gave a half shrug and opened the door. Oh, well. Maybe Brody was scolding Levine for letting her slip away from his man this morning. She would have to remember to tell Brody to deal more gently with Barry. The poor man had been having a difficult time of it since she had appeared on the scene.

Lunch. Sandwiches seemed entirely too commonplace today, when she felt like a celebration. Perhaps she would make a salmon crepe. If Brody was truly hungry, she could fix him a few canapés to hold him over until the culinary masterpiece.

She shut the door and hurried down the hall toward the kitchen, trying to recall the recipe for the cream sauce for the crepes.

"What are all these?" Sacha gazed in astonishment as Harris set down two large pigskin suitcases in the foyer.

"Your luggage." Brody strolled forward to stand beside her. "How many more bags are there, Harris?"

"Three suitcases and one overnighter." Harris said with a grin. "I'll be back in a minute. You want them in the master bedroom?"

Brody nodded. "We'll unpack them later."

Harris nodded as he turned to go. "Right you are."

"Unpack?" Sacha pulled her gaze away from Harris's departing figure and lifted it to Brody's face.

"I called a shop in Rodeo Drive and had them send out a few things for you to wear. You said you had to leave Paris with practically nothing."

"A *few* things. Five suitcases constitutes more than a bare minimum, I would say." There was a caustic edge to her words. "It borders on the ridiculous."

"Well, I actually prefer you in the bare minimum, but I decided not to indulge myself. It's very bad for my character." His light eyes twinkled down at her. "After all, letting you get dressed occasionally might make the other times more titillating."

The color rose to her cheeks. It was true neither of them had been overly concerned with clothes for the past twenty-four hours. After they had returned from the theater yesterday afternoon, Brody had not only failed to do justice to her wonderful lunch, he had ignored it altogether, whisking her off to the bedroom with a practiced seductive skill that had set her head spinning and her heart pounding. There had been an almost frantic urgency about his lovemaking that had puzzled her at first. Later she had not been able to think at all as he wove about her a fiery web of sensuality that excluded everything but sensation. "I don't think you have need of titillation," she said dryly. "And I will not take these clothes."

His smile faded. "Why not?"

She made an impatient gesture with one hand. "It's impossible. Like something from a romance novel. Gestures like this . . . It's too much."

"Heaven knows I don't pretend to be a hero from a romance novel." Brody's lips tightened. "Who should know better than you that the superstar has feet of clay? It's only a present, for heaven's sake."

"It would smother me. I told you I couldn't bear to take—"

"I *liked* you in that blue velvet robe," he said, his expression growing stormy. "I wanted to see you in something besides jeans and Donald Duck T-shirts. I bought them for *me*, dammit."

"Then I'm sure they're definitely the wrong size and that they wouldn't suit you at all."

"Sacha . . ." Exasperation turned into a flare of anger. "All right. Let's put this on a strictly business level. You don't seem to know how to accept a gift graciously." He was speaking through clenched teeth. "Marceline's women are fifteen hundred dollars a night, base price. I figure yesterday afternoon at the theater should count for at least one night. Then there was last night. That's three thousand dollars. Of course, some of the things we did would have cost me extra. Say, four thousand." He grabbed her wrist and strode down the hall, pulling her behind him. "Does that coincide with your figures?"

"Yes . . . no . . ." Sacha stammered. "Where are we going?"

"The guest room. Harris will be taking the bags to the master suite, and we don't want to be interrupted." He threw open the door, jerked her into the room, and slammed the door. "I don't know how much those damn clothes cost, and I certainly wouldn't want you to feel in debt. I'd say another six or seven hours in the sack ought to do it. If you're lucky, I'll be the one owing you."

"Why are you so angry?" she whispered.

"Because you're *cheating* me." His eyes blazed into her own. "You're stealing the pleasure I would have gotten from giving to you. You're always talking about giving. What about me? I've been a selfish bastard all my life, and never even wanted to give to anyone before. It's the first time for me, and I have to pick a woman who records everything in credit and debit columns. Well, what are you waiting for? Take off your clothes."

She was gazing at him in surprise. Her fingers automatically moved to unbutton her blouse. "Very well."

"You'd do it." He jerked her hand away from her blouse. "Over a bunch of stupid rags. What kind of man do you think I am that I'd make you— Why the hell are you laughing? It's not funny, dammit."

Her eyes were dancing. "Oh, but it is." Her fingers reached up to touch the broad plane of his cheek. "Brody, I'll take the 'stupid rags,' and I absolutely refuse to pay for them on my back. Are you satisfied?"

"You're not just saying that?" he asked suspiciously.

She held up her hand. "No, truly. What is more, I refuse to cook you even one meal to pay for them."

He began to relax. "Not even one meal? I may have created a monster."

"Too late." Her finger moved down to trace the clean cut of his lips. "I may even decide to demand more from you. Perhaps a new Mercedes or a Rolls-Royce."

"Why?" he asked softly, his gaze searching her face. "Why, Sacha?"

"Because you're right. I am selfish. I never realized how selfish I was being before." Her eyes were thoughtful. "It is a joy to me to give to people, and yet I refused to accept gifts from anyone else." Her expression became grave. "It will not be easy for me; I'll probably backslide quite often."

"I'll break you in easy. We'll skip the Rolls."

She laughed huskily as she nodded. "I probably wouldn't have time to drive it during the short time I'll be here anyway."

His smile vanished. "That's right, you wouldn't. I forgot for the moment this was only a temporary arrangement." He took her hand from his mouth and lingeringly kissed the palm. "So why don't you get undressed?"

She grinned. "I'm afraid to waste my time. You can't seem to make up your mind on that score."

"It's made up now." There was a flicker of pain in his face before he smiled. "I'd be a fool not to take advantage of our time together, wouldn't I? We've already discussed what a valuable commodity you are."

Sacha's smile faded. Yes, and she would also be a fool. These were golden moments, perhaps the only ones she'd ever know. Giving, taking, what difference did it make? In years to come the shards of memory would all mellow and merge into one halcyon whole. She smiled tenderly as she resumed unbuttoning her blouse. "And I'm only a beginner. I'm sure I'll increase in value with experience." She shrugged out of the blouse and tossed it on the chair beside the bed. "And with your expert tutelage, of course."

"Of course," he repeated lightly as he took a step closer. Yet there was nothing light in the expression in his eyes, they held only gravity, tenderness, and a strange melancholy. "My poor talents are always at your disposal, milady."

And his hands gently cupped her naked breasts.

"A sand dune!" Sacha laughed delightedly as she ran toward the knoll that had been tinted a rose-beige hue in the last light of the setting sun.

She glanced over her shoulder, her eyes dancing with mischief. "I seem to recall you saying something about a sand dune." She tilted her head and pretended to think. "Now, what was it?"

"It would be better for both of us if you forget that particular fantasy until we get back to the house," Brody said dryly. "Levine and his men are watching our every move, and I find I'm not as much of an exhibitionist as I thought." He paused. "Not with you."

Her eyes softened. "Good. I like that." She threw herself down on the sand, leaned back against the dune's cushioning softness, and sighed with contentment. "Though I'll admit you draw a very exciting word picture, I would not like to share our lovemaking. Particularly since Barry is such a camera bug."

Brody became still. "Camera bug?"

"Yes, didn't you notice? He's been shooting pictures of us ever since we started walking on the beach."

Brody's eyes shifted to the scarlet and mauve brilliance of the sunset. "I guess I didn't pay any attention."

Sacha chuckled. "Maybe he takes pictures of all his famous clients as old-age insurance. Someday he'll probably write a book—*Bodyguard to the Stars*—and make a million dollars."

"I doubt it. Randal makes his men sign an oath of confidentiality that probably precludes exposés. It's more likely just a hobby." He reached down and pulled her to her feet. "Come on. I'm hungry. Let's go back to the house and I'll cook dinner."

"*You* cook?"

"Why not? I don't have any hang-ups about keeping women in the kitchen." A tiny smile tugged at his lips. "And since your declaration of independence, I'd be afraid to ask you to be chef."

"But I *like* to cook. I'm a wonderful cook."

He gave a mock martyr's sigh. "Very well, if you insist. I'll make the supreme sacrifice and just sit and watch."

She made a face at him. "Oh, no. You have a wonderful talent also. While you're sitting watching me cook you can work on it."

He gazed at her warily. "Work on what?"

"That sand-dune fantasy. I think, if you tried, you could embellish it with all kinds of interesting highlights and variations for me. It might be very exciting." She frowned sternly. "But for later. We must not waste another meal. It will be something to look forward to after dinner."

A faint smile tugged at his lips. "Like dessert?"

She nodded. "Exactly like dessert."

His laughter rang out over the beach as his hand tightened on hers and they started toward the steps leading to the house on the cliff.

Nine

The pistol shone with a deadly cold luster in the soft diffusion of the lamplight.

Sacha gazed with shock at the gun in the drawer of the bedside table. It was as if she had opened the drawer to see a snake coiled and ready to strike. She reached out a tentative finger to touch the mother-of-pearl handle.

"Sacha, where did you put—" Brody stopped, pausing in the doorway of the bathroom wearing only a towel knotted around his hips, his chest-nut hair water-darkened to deep brown from the shower. "Don't touch it. I'm not sure the safety is on."

She jerked her hand back as it had been burned. "I was looking for a nail file. I thought I saw one in here this morning." She turned slowly to look at him. "There was no gun in this drawer then."

"No, there wasn't." Brody came forward and decisively shut the drawer. "I asked Levine to give me a few guns for the house. There's also one in the cutlery drawer of the kitchen cabinet and another in the hall closet." He smiled. "Just so you don't receive any more unpleasant surprises."

"Three guns." She shook her head dazedly. "Why so many? Why even one? You have all those guards outside. There's no chance anyone could get inside." Her eyes widened in sudden alarm. "Or is there?"

"I just like to be on the safe side." He didn't look at her as he turned back toward the bathroom. "Where did you put the hair dryer? I can't find the damn thing."

"In the bottom drawer of the vanity." She followed him across the bedroom. "But why now? We've been here three days, and there has been no sign of Gino. Why would you want to make the house an armed camp?"

"Three guns don't make an armed camp." Brody plugged the hair dryer into the socket on the wall beside the vanity. "Why don't you make us an Irish coffee? I liked that touch of cinnamon you used—"

"Why are you always sending me off to cook when you want to distract me?" She came forward into the bathroom and unplugged the hair dryer. "And you should not use electrical appliances in the bathroom. I read an article that said many people are electrocuted while using hair dryers near water. That's why I put it in the bottom drawer. We will buy you a portable one that runs on batteries."

A smile curved his lips. "Yes, ma'am. Is it all right if I use it in the bedroom?"

"Of course." She felt a melting deep inside as she looked at him. That lazily mischievous smile should be against the law, Sacha told herself. "In fact, I will do it for you. Remember, you dried my hair one night?"

"Oh, yes, I remember." He pulled a face. "And it nearly drove me insane." His voice lowered to velvet sexuality. "I'll be delighted to return the favor."

The melting began to ignite tiny languid flames in every vein. "I didn't mean to—" She broke off. "You're doing it again. No Irish coffee and no seduction. Not until you answer my questions."

He lifted a brow. "Want to bet?"

She took a hasty step backward. "No, Brody, you aren't being fair. I'm truly concerned about this. That gun frightened me."

He studied her thoughtfully. "All right." He turned away and laid the hair dryer on the counter of the vanity. "Dammit, I was hoping to put this off until tomorrow morning. There's an evening newspaper in the second drawer of the desk in the study. You'd better take a look at it."

She gazed at him in bewilderment and then turned on her heel and left the bathroom.

Brody ran a comb through his damp hair, took off the towel, and slipped on his terry-cloth robe before following her to the study.

Sacha was gazing at the picture in the gossip

section of the newspaper. "It's a shot of you and me on the beach." She lifted her gaze. "Levine?"

He nodded. "I told him to take a few pictures of us together and then feed them to the columnists, making sure there was a caption mentioning where they'd been taken."

"I guess I don't have to ask why. A trap?"

"It has to end. Louis said that and I agree. You'll be in danger until it does."

"Well, you certainly laid a clear trail for him." Her hands were trembling as they held the newspaper, and she deliberately steadied them. "You did everything but give him the exact address and spread out the welcome mat." She closed her eyes. "Dear heaven, I wish you hadn't done this thing."

He took a step closer and gently took the paper from her. "It has to end," he repeated. "Don't be afraid, I won't let anything happen to you."

"Afraid?" Her lashes flew open to reveal eyes shimmering with tears. "Of course, I'm afraid. What a stupid thing to do. He's going to come here. Gino is going to come *here*. Until you did this, there was a chance he wouldn't find us."

"I told you that I'll keep you safe. I know you don't like being bait but—"

"Do you think I'm afraid for myself? What kind of person do you think I am? Gino almost killed you the other night. This time he'll probably succeed. Don't you understand? He doesn't care whether people live or die if they get in his way." She rubbed her ear. "He laughs—"

"Shh. . . ." He took her hand from her ear and brought it to his cheek. "He's not going to hurt anyone again. If Amanti gets out of this alive, he'll be put away for a long, long time on an attempted homicide charge. I've set Randal investigating him too. He'll dig up everything illegal Gino's ever done in his life." He turned his head, and his lips touched her palm. "But we have to catch him first."

She jerked her hand away. "Stop being so damn soothing. If you think I'm going to stay here and lure him to your house, you're insane." She whirled away from him. "I won't—"

He grabbed her shoulders and turned her back to face him. "You will," he said with implacable firmness. "You're not going anywhere, Sacha. You're through running away."

"I won't stay here," she said, blazing with anger. "You broke our agreement. You said you'd make sure you'd be safe here. I would never have come if I'd known you'd do something like this."

He shook her gently. "Stop it. We're long past agreements and bargains." He forced her to look into his eyes. "Aren't we, Sacha?"

"No, I . . ." She drew a shaky breath. "Yes, but you had no right to do this."

"Perhaps, but it's done now, and the trap is set. Levine and his men are deployed undercover outside and won't make a move until Gino is inside the house. Levine has set up a radio signal that will set off a beeper he gave me if any intruder is sighted on the grounds." His mouth tightened. "And if you try to leave, Levine will escort you politely but firmly back to the house."

Her eyes widened. "You'd keep me prisoner?"

"I don't want to do it."

"But you would. I don't like this, Brody."

A flicker of pain crossed his face. "Do you think I do? I'm scared to death I've set you up as bait, and something will happen to you. But I'm more scared of letting you run away with no protection. You can't leave, Sacha."

"Don't count on it." She took his hands from her shoulders. "I developed a violent antipathy to coercion when I was a child. I won't be anyone's prisoner, not even yours, Brody."

"It will only be for a little while."

She shook her head. "No! You've made a mistake but I won't compound it by remaining here. I'll find a way to get away from Levine *and* you." She turned and strode out of the study.

"Peace offering." Brody stood in the doorway of the bedrooms holding a tray containing two tall cups frothed with tiny mountains of whipped cream. "*I* made the Irish coffee." A worried frown creased his forehead. "I may have gone overboard on the cinnamon though." He crossed the room and sat down on the bed beside her. Balancing the tray precariously in one hand, he awkwardly plumped up her pillows with the other. "That's a pretty nightgown. I told the shop to send something blue." A teasing smile touched his lips. "Now that I think about it, I've never seen you in any of those nightgowns. I wonder why?"

He knew very well why, Sacha thought crossly. Their passion for each other had been too urgent to allow them to tolerate even a wisp of material between them. "Why are you here? I'm very displeased with you, Brody."

His smile faded. "I know. That's why I'm here." He gazed at her soberly. "We may not be together much longer, and I don't want to waste a moment on bitterness." He took a cup off the tray and offered it to her. "Peace, Sacha?"

A wrenching pain tore through her. He was right. One way or the other their time together was coming to an end. How would she be able to bear it? He was so dear. Passion and wicked mischief. Gentleness and humor. Arrogance and insecurity. He was a paradox of characteristics that only made him more human and lovable. She couldn't stay here and put him in danger, but they need not part in anger.

She took the cup from him and smiled. "Peace."

He breathed a sigh of relief that was almost boyish. "Good." He set the tray on the bedside table and took his own cup from it. He took a tentative sip. "Too much cinnamon?"

She took a drink of the coffee. Far too much cinnamon. But how could she tell him when he was gazing at her so hopefully? "It's wonderful. Better than mine?"

He chuckled. "Now I know I'm forgiven. You're lying to me."

"No, truly, it's—" She met his eyes and burst out laughing. "Almost tolerable."

He looked down at the whipped cream in his cup. "Have I ever told you how I love to hear you laugh? It's always rich and earthy and makes me want to laugh too."

She took another sip. "Even when it's so unkind as to be at your fine coffee?"

"Even then," he said thickly. He raised his gaze. "I don't mind. I like it. Everyone takes me so damn seriously. The so-called great actor, Brody Devlin. Even Cass does it sometimes. You're the only one who really laughs at me."

"I take you seriously too." She reached out a hand to ruffle his chestnut hair as if he were a small boy. "But life is too short for us to go around with long faces. I have to laugh." She brought the cup to her lips again. "And besides, I was laughing at your coffee, not you."

He stopped her before she could take another sip. "Well, I won't make you suffer any longer. You've had enough of the stuff to soothe my ego."

She brushed his hand aside. "I'm getting accustomed to it. Maybe I'll use an entire box of cinnamon, too, from now on." She lifted the cup to her lips again.

"I said, you've had enough!"

Her eyes widened at the sharpness of his voice.

He smiled with an effort as he took the cup from her hand and set it and his own cup on the tray. "You're tired. Go to sleep. I'll take the tray back to the kitchen."

She *was* suddenly sleepy, a peculiar heavy drowsiness.

Brody's gaze was narrowed on her with a watchfulness that was also odd. Why was he . . . ? Then she knew!

Her gaze flew to the cup on the tray. "You *drugged* me."

He nodded. "Only a light sedative. It was necessary, Sacha."

"Necessary." The word sounded slurred even to her own ears. "How could you do such a thing?"

His hand gently brushed her hair back; his face was a mask of pain. "I know you, Sacha. You would have made a run for it. I couldn't let you do that. And you would never have gone along with the rest of the plan."

"What are you talking about?"

"The trap's been baited. Gino knows where you are. There's no need for you to stay here now. I'm moving you to a house about a mile down the beach and sending some men to guard you."

She felt panicky even though sedated. "But if he thinks I'm here, he'll come. You'll be alone."

He nodded grimly. "And waiting."

"He'll kill you." She struggled to sit up, but her muscles felt too heavy to move. "No, Brody, please."

He leaned forward and gently brushed her forehead with his lips. "Don't fight the sedative, Sacha. I'll be fine. I've played in enough thrillers to be at least adequate at the role. I won't let anything happen to me. Just relax and go to sleep. When you wake, it will all be over and you'll be safe."

"No, Brody, you don't know him. He'll—"

A shrill buzz interrupted her words, and Brody

stiffened as if he'd been stabbed. "No! No! Not *now*, dammit!"

The buzz was repeated, and Brody reached into the pocket of his robe and took out a small rectangular control box. He pressed a button and then jammed the box back into his pocket. He got up from the bed, reached into the drawer of the bedside table, and drew out the gun Sacha had discovered earlier in the evening. "Sacha, listen to me." He wrapped her hand around the mother-of-pearl handle of the gun. "Try to stay awake."

He had just told her to go to sleep, she thought hazily. Why couldn't he make up his mind?

"He's coming, Sacha. I wanted to get you away from here before he—" He drew a deep breath. "I'm going to the kitchen and get the other gun. He'll have to come in through either the kitchen or the front door. I'm going to stop him." He moistened his lips. "But if something goes wrong, you've got to stay awake so that you'll be able to protect yourself. All you have to do is point the gun and pull the trigger. Okay?" He leaned forward and gave her a quick hard kiss. "It's going to be all right." Then he was gone.

If something went wrong. What had he meant? Gino. . . . If something went wrong, Brody would die. He had given her the gun to protect herself, and he had no weapon. "No!"

She struggled to a sitting position, her hand clutching the handle of the gun. She hadn't realized such a small pistol could be so heavy. Her wrists felt as if they were made of water, but she must hold onto it. Brody needed the gun.

She swung her legs to the floor and swayed dizzily. Damn Brody. Why had he done this to her? He had wanted to protect her. King Arthur to the rescue, sacrificing everything with a gallantry he hadn't even known he possessed.

She was on her feet, walking toward the door. Waves of darkness kept coming in and going out like a capricious tide. She clutched the jamb of the door, feeling a vague sense of triumph. She had made it to the first goal, now she had only to get down the hall and—

A crash!

Another crash. And then the sounds of curses from the direction of the kitchen! She knew that voice. "Gino." She didn't know she had whispered the name. Gino was in the house. Brody hadn't been able to reach the gun in the kitchen in time. Another crash. They were fighting! Brody's voice, reverberating down the hall, jarring her from the horrified haze, encapsulating her.

She was running down the hall. At least she thought she was running. She seemed to be moving in slow motion. Then suddenly she was standing in the doorway of the kitchen.

Gino. Just the same as in years past. A mountain of a man with thick curly black hair and beard and a face that had haunted her life since she was seven years old. Gino and Brody were on the floor struggling. But Gino was so strong. She knew how strong he was. She had to stop it.

"Gino." He didn't hear her. She repeated it, louder. "Gino, I'm here. It's me you want."

He looked up, and a savage smile of joy lit his face. "Pretty little Sacha." He tore free of Brody's hold and rolled away. "Oh, yes. It's you I want. I've had ten years to think how much I want you."

"Sacha, get out of here." Brody's voice betrayed the agony he was feeling. "He has a knife."

She saw it now, gleaming wickedly in Gino's left hand. But why was Brody so frightened for her when she had a gun in her own hand? She glanced down and realized that her gun was hidden by the floating skirt of her gown. She tried to lift it, but it was too heavy. She would try again in a moment when she had gathered more strength. "He likes knives," she said dully. "Almost as much as cigars. Right, Gino?"

"Ah, you remember." Gino got to his knees. "You were a very brave child. I almost hated to hurt you like that."

Brody was fading back toward the cabinet, taking advantage of Gino's concentration on Sacha. The cutlery drawer, she realized. He was trying to reach the gun in the cutlery drawer. She had to keep Gino's attention, but it was so hard to think. "I was afraid of you. We were all afraid of you, Gino. Did it make you happy knowing you could make a child fear you?"

"As a matter of fact, it did." Gino rose to his feet, his enormous bulk suddenly dominating the small kitchen. "It made me feel a little godlike. I was the 'boss.' The money was good, but that feeling was better." The knife glittered in his hand as he stood there, his eyes narrowed on her. "I could throw this knife, Sacha, and pierce your heart. Or I could come closer and feel it sink into your flesh. Which should I do, pretty Sacha?"

From the corner of her eye she saw that Brody had reached the cutlery drawer. She tried to keep her gaze fixed on Gino's face. "You never let us choose before. Why now, Gino?"

"You're right." Gino's deep laugh boomed out. "I want to *feel* you die." He began to come toward her.

She lifted the gun in her hand and pointed it at him, trying desperately to stop it from wobbling.

The next few moments were a jumble of wild impressions: Gino's arm drawing back to hurl the knife. Levine's shout as he and his men rushed into the room. Brody's cry of rage and panic. A shot tearing through the room. Gino's look of surprise as he fell to his knees and slumped over. Had she shot him?

Then she was falling, the shining beige tile of the floor rising up to meet her. "Brody!" Was Brody all right? She couldn't see him in the darkness. "Brody, where are you?"

She heard a low sob as strong arms closed around her. Then she heard nothing at all as the darkness deepened into unconsciousness.

Ten

Cass Radison was sitting in the chair beside the bed and smiling down at her.

Cass? Something was wrong. Cass wasn't supposed to be here in Malibu. He had returned to his own apartment in Los Angeles. Sacha shook her head to clear it of the fuzziness clouding her thinking.

"It's all right." Cass leaned forward and spoke quickly. "Everything's fine. Just relax, Sacha."

Relax. That was what Brody had told her after she had found out he had put the sedative in her coffee. Brody! She sat bolt upright in bed. "Gino! Is Brody all right?"

"Brody's fine," Cass said soothingly. "And you weren't hurt either. Brody stopped Gino before he could throw the knife."

She lifted a shaking hand to push back her

hair. "I was going to shoot him but the gun was too heavy."

"Brody shot him."

Her gaze met Cass's. "Is Gino dead?"

Cass shook his head. "No. But he won't be out of the hospital for quite a while, and after that he'll face a damn long prison sentence. Randal uncovered a rather nasty murder Gino Amanti was connected with about fifteen years ago."

"I see." Gino was out of her life. How strange it felt. Free, but strange. She couldn't quite comprehend it. "How long have I been asleep?"

"Almost twelve hours. Brody asked me to stay with you to explain everything and go over the arrangements."

"Arrangements?"

He nodded as he took out a small notebook and flicked it open. "He wants you to stay here as long as you like, and I'm to invite Benoit to be his guest here too. In case you wish to return to Paris, he owns a villa just outside the city, and the same arrangement could exist there. There will be a generous monthly allowance, of course, but he has a good deal of influence in this city, and he thinks he could pull certain strings to help your career. Harris will stay with you as long as you need him and—"

"Stop!" She held up her hand. Her head was whirling with confusion. "What are you talking about? I can't take any of these things."

"He was very specific," Cass said gently. "He wants to make sure you're safe—and happy. He said to tell you that he wants you *happy*, not content, whatever that means to the two of you. Something about rockets going off and a 'shining.' "

"Why are you telling me all this?" she whispered. "Why doesn't Brody tell me himself?"

Cass hesitated. "He's not here, Sacha."

Pain. White-hot agonizing pain. "Where is he?"

"He just left in a taxi for the airport. He's on the four o'clock flight on TWA to New York."

"He's going so he can do the play," she said numbly.

"I'm not sure," Cass said. "He just told me he was going to New York, and that I should make sure you were well taken care of."

"Just like that? Without waiting to say goodbye or letting me thank him for all he's done for me?"

"You can't say he didn't think about you. These are very generous arrangements."

"Oh, yes, very generous." Her hands clenched on the coverlet. "Did he actually think I'd accept his fine 'arrangements'?"

He pulled a face. "It's my job to make sure you do."

"Then you're not going to succeed at your job," she said shakily. "He can take his arrangements and—" Her voice broke, and she took a deep quivering breath. "Why? Why would he leave without seeing me?"

"I don't know, Sacha. He's a complicated man, and he can be pretty inscrutable when he wants to be." He paused. "But don't think it was easy for him. I know Brody well enough to realize he was hurting."

"Hurting!" Her eyes were suddenly blazing. "Well, I'm sorry he's hurting, but I'm hurting too." She threw the coverlet aside and swung her feet to the floor. "And I deserve better than this. At least he should have let me say good-bye. He shot a man for my sake, he set me free, and now he just walks away without even giving me a chance to thank him." She glanced at the clock on the bedside table. One fifteen. There was still time. She jumped to her feet and walked quickly toward the bathroom. "Tell Harris I'll want the car in fifteen minutes."

"Where are you going?"

"The airport. How can I find him there?"

"He'll probably be in the VIP Lounge, but—"

The bathroom door slammed shut behind her.

Sacha threw open the paneled teak door of the VIP Lounge and strode into the deep carpeted luxury of the room.

A pretty uniformed woman sitting at an elegant desk by the door gave Sacha's shabby, jean-clad figure one swift glance and rose hastily to her feet. "I'm sorry, but these are private rooms, and I'm afraid—"

"Hush," Sacha said impatiently, her gaze traveling swiftly around the tastefully decorated lounge. "I will not be here long."

"But this is a—"

Sacha stopped listening as she caught sight of Brody across the room standing looking out of a large picture window. His back was turned to her but there was no mistaking that lithe muscular grace of his. She started toward him, swiftly covering the distance separating them.

The receptionist raised her voice. "You have to have special permission. You can't—"

"Watch me." Sacha didn't spare the woman another glance. "Brody!"

She saw Brody stiffen as her voice carried to him. He turned slowly to confront her. His face was pale, shuttered, as his brilliant blue gaze flicked over her. "Hello, Sacha. I hoped to avoid this."

She stopped before him. "I know you did, but I'm not going to let you do it." She tilted back her head to look him in the eyes. "I'm angry with you. You hurt me very much."

He flinched. "I did more than hurt you. I almost got you killed. I guess I'm better at pretense than real life. I thought you'd want to see the back of me."

"Nonsense. You thought no such thing. You were afraid I'd treat you to a tearful scene and embarrass you. You should have known I wouldn't do that." Her lips were trembling. "But I had to say good-bye." She held out her hand. "Thank you for freeing me from Gino and being so patient with my foolishness when I thought you were my—" Her voice was becoming shaky, and she had to stop for a moment before she could go on. "Good-bye, Brody."

Brody's eyes were glittering as he took her hand. "Dear God, how I wish you hadn't come here."

"I will go away soon."

His hand tightened on hers. "Sacha . . ."

"You'll be magnificent in the play."

"I'm not sure I'm going to do it. I just wanted to—"

"Get away from me?" Her lips tightened with pain. "You know I wouldn't bother you."

"Bother me?" He laughed huskily. "When have you ever done anything else? You've turned my life upside down. I don't even know who I am anymore."

"You are a fine man and a great actor." She pulled her hand away. She had to get away from here before she exploded with pain. "Have a good life, Brody." She turned and started to walk away from him.

"Take care of yourself, Sacha," Brody called softly after her. Then, in a tone scarcely above a whisper. "I love you."

She stopped, frozen in place. "What did you say?"

Brody didn't answer.

She whirled to face him. No words were necessary; it was there in his face. "You love me," she said clearly. "And you're doing something as stupid as *leaving* me?" She strode back toward him. "I cannot believe you'd be so idiotic. Perhaps I don't understand you. Perhaps you love me as a friend. Like I love Louis."

"Yes, I love you as a friend."

Her gaze searched his face. "Bah, you lie, Brody. You love me as I love you." Her face was suddenly illuminated with joy as she swept into his arms and hugged him with all her strength. "You love my body and my soul and what we are together and apart. You love *me*."

Brody's arms closed around her, and he buried his face in her hair. "Sacha, don't do this to me. I'm trying to do the right thing. Do you know how hard it was to leave you? You know how selfish I am. I wanted to reach out and hold on forever. But you don't need me. You're young and bright, and every day is the start of a new adventure for you. You can find someone else who can share those adventures."

She stepped back. "But I want to share those adventures with you."

"I'm selfish and self-centered and insecure. I'm probably even a little neurotic; most actors are. You don't want to spend your life with someone like me."

"Yes, I do. Even neurotic actors need love." She laughed. "And I need you, Brody."

He frowned. "I've made sure you're secure. You don't need anyone."

"Then why did I feel as if you'd stabbed me to the heart when Cass told me you had gone? Why am I so happy now I want to dance on tables and hug that silly girl at the reception desk? I love you and you love me, and we're going to have a wonderful life together. Trust me."

He shook his head. "I'm not right for you." His

expression turned somber. "And someday you'll find that out and leave me. I don't think that I could take that, Sacha."

She gazed at him, an expression of loving exasperation on her face. Why couldn't he believe in himself as much as she did in him? "Brody Devlin, you—" She framed his face in her two hands. "Listen to me. I'm not ever going to leave you. Why should I? You're loving, gentle, sexy. You're my brother and friend, King Arthur and Lancelot. I know all your faults and I accept them, just as you must accept mine. We'll try to correct our faults, but even if we don't, the love will still be there."

He bent his head to kiss her lingeringly. "I do love you, Sacha," he whispered. "I shouldn't let you do this, but I don't think I can ever let you go. I'd die if you left me now. You've made me come alive. You called me a spellbinder, but you're the one who has the magic."

"Then why do you doubt that I can perform this paltry little trick?" Her eyes twinkled up at him. "It should be very simple. Poof. Abracadabra. Henceforth Brody and Sacha will be joined together for the rest of their lives. There. It is done."

Brody chuckled, his face alight with joy and tenderness as he looked down into her eyes. "And they lived happily ever after."

THE EDITOR'S CORNER

I AM DELIGHTED TO WELCOME KATE HARTSON AS YOUR AUTHOR OF THIS MONTH'S EDITOR'S CORNER, AND TO LET YOU KNOW THAT NORA ROBERTS'S NEXT SIZZLING ROMANTIC SUSPENSE NOVEL—**SACRED SINS**—WILL COME OUT NEXT MONTH.

HAPPY HOLIDAYS!

Carolyn Nichols

I'm delighted to have joined the LOVESWEPT team as Senior Editor to work on these fabulous romances, and I'm glad to be writing the Editor's Corner this month so that I can say *hi* to all of you.

Isn't it a treat having six LOVESWEPT books every month? We never have to be without a LOVESWEPT in the bedroom, den, or purse. And now there are enough of these luscious stories to last through the month!

Soon we'll be rushing into the holiday season, full of sharing and good cheer. We have some special LOVESWEPT books to share—our holiday gifts to you!

RAINBOW RYDER, LOVESWEPT #222, by Linda Hampton, is a gift of excitement, as our respectable heroine, Kathryn Elizabeth Asbury, a pillar of the community, finds herself attracted to Ryder Malone, a wildly handsome rogue who has a penchant for riding motorcycles. Kathryn's orderly life is shaken by Ryder, who isn't quite what he appears to be. She fights hard for control

(continued)

but really can't resist this wild and free-spirited "King of the Road." Then she makes a thrilling discovery—and falling hard doesn't hurt a bit. **RAINBOW RYDER** is sure to be one of your favorites, but don't stop reading, we have five more LOVESWEPT GIFTS for you. . . .

Diamonds are the gift in Glenna McReynolds's **THIEVES IN THE NIGHT,** LOVESWEPT #223—how appropriate for the holiday season! Our heroine, Chantal Cochard, is an ex-jewel thief forced out of retirement when her family's prize diamond necklace shows up around some other woman's neck. DIAMONDS may be a girl's best friend, but they're not her lover. That's better left to well-built, sexy men like our hero, Jaz Peterson. Once Chantal invites him into her Aspen hideaway, she quickly learns that love is the most precious jewel of all!

Witty Linda Cajio's gift to us is **DOUBLE DEALING,** LOVESWEPT #224, a story of childhood dreams and adult surrender. Our heroine, Rae Varkely, mistress of a fabulous estate, is forced into a position where she simply has to kidnap Jed Waters. She makes a ransom demand, but our hero refuses to be released! Making demands of his own, he turns the tables on Rae, who can't help but pay with her heart. Still she has to protect her property from Jed's plans for development. But Jed has no intention of destroying anything—he only wants to build a strong relationship with the mistress of the manor.

A new book from Kay Hooper is always a gift, but **ZACH'S LAW,** LOVESWEPT #225, is an especially wonderful one. As the tale continues of those incredible men who work for Joshua Logan (and who indirectly fall out of SERENA'S WEB), we meet petite Teddy Tyler stranded on a deserted mountain road. Zach Steele, a strong, silent type who frightens Teddy because he ignites such strong desire in her, is her rescuer . . . then her sweet jailer . . . and the captive of her love. But Hagen's got his claws into Zach, there's mayhem on the horizon, and there's Zach's own past to confront before true love can win out!

(continued)

Sara Orwig's **OUT OF A MIST,** LOVESWEPT #226, is a gift of desire, as Millie and Ken are reunited after a brief but unforgettable encounter. Ken is on the run from the law, and Millie discovers him wounded and hiding in her closet. Of course, she knows he's done nothing wrong and she lets him stay with her until they can clear his name. But the longer he stays, the more he finds a place in her heart. Millie blossoms in Ken's embrace, but Ken won't settle for just passion—his desire is the lasting kind!

Our final romantic gift for you is a wonderful new book by Patt Buchiester called **TWO ROADS,** LOVESWEPT #227. This moving book is a story of healing: Nicole Piccolo is recovering from a broken leg and a broken heart, trying to forget Clay Masters, the man who promised her *forever* and then disappeared from her life. When Clay reappears a year later, the wounds are opened again, but Clay is determined to show Nicole that he never meant to leave and his heart has always been hers. When the healing is complete, they begin again with no pain to mar the exquisite pleasure of being in love.

Enjoy our gifts to you, sent with love and good cheer from your LOVESWEPT authors and editors!

Kate Hartson

Kate Hartson
  Editor
LOVESWEPT
Bantam Books, Inc.
666 Fifth Avenue
New York, NY 10103